A Desert Rivalry

A Hearts of Woolsey Novel - Book 3

Savannah Hendricks

Grand Bayou Press

Library of Congress Control Number: 2022916820

ISBN Paperback 978-1-7344553-6-6

eBook B09P6PK6SR

For Film and TV Rights – GrandBayouPress@protonmail.com

Editor: Krista Dapkey - www.kdproofreading.com

A DESERT RIVALRY

Contents

For Linda Martin -
Even Christmas needs a dinosaur.

Welcome to Woolsey

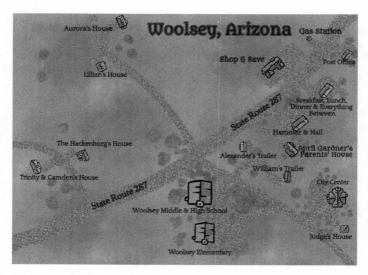

Cast of Characters
Alexander Adams - librarian
April Gardner - temporary librarian

A DESERT RIVALRY

Elizabeth Dunn - Judge
William Adams - Alexander's dad
Lillian Taylor - Trinity's Mom
Charlie Tow - owns Shop & Save
Sydney Hernandez - post office employee
Gavin Hart - long time neighbor of Mama & Elizabeth
Aurora Easton - Trinity's best friend
Mike Easton - Aurora's husband
Willa Easton - daughter to Aurora & Mike
Ava Easton - daughter to Aurora & Mike
Trinity Moore - teacher
Camden Moore - teacher
Jolie Moore – Trinity & Camden's daughter
R. J. Smith - owns Hammer & Nail
Ezra Hackenberg - firefighter
Wyatt Hackenberg - firefighter
Jasmine & Jeter Hackenberg - Ezra & Wyatt's children

Chapter 1

Alexander

"Dr. Wagner, I find this news unacceptable," Alexander Adams stated.

The thin paper that covered the exam table in the doctor's office stuck to the back of his bare legs, and sweat caused by apprehension formed across Alexander's back.

"Unacceptable or not, if you don't have the surgery, you won't be able to keep working at the library, or anywhere for that matter." Dr. Wagner sat on a circular stool as he typed into the laptop that he rested on his knees.

"You said it's outpatient surgery, which means I should be back at work the next day. I'll rest the day of and be careful afterward. I have to set the library up for its annual LCC."

The doctor looked up from the laptop, his eyes questioning Alexander.

"The Library's Christmas Celebration."

Dr. Wagner nodded. "You won't be able to lift anything for a few weeks, and you'll need at least a month of physical therapy once I've cleared it."

"Dr. Wagner, I'm the town's only librarian."

"That's right. You live in that tiny town out west."

"Tiny is relative. Square mileage-wise, Woolsey is rather large. However, you can refer to the population as tiny."

Dr. Wagner stood up, the laptop still open, resting on his palm. "Close up the library for a few days; the town will be fine. Or maybe hire a temp."

"A stranger in my library . . . using my desk?"

"Not a stranger, someone in town who can cover for you. Remember—no heavy lifting. *Especially* stacks of books. Good thing there're e-books."

Alexander's mouth fell far enough open it almost tapped against his chest. "Electronic books?"

Dr. Wagner shook his head and opened the door to the hall. "My receptionist will have your surgery information and schedule. Be sure to check with her on your way out. See you soon, Alexander."

As the door shut, Alexander stared down at the tops of his bare legs, their back sides remained stuck to the tissue paper. He closed his eyes and envisioned the library. Alexander needed to trust his doctor's advice, at least for the surgery, but he was unsure about everything else. Dr. Wagner might be a well-educated doctor, but his stance on electronic books was not related to his career—being able to swipe a page with one finger . . . ludicrous. Although there was no one to see him, the notion sent Alexander's head into an automatic shake of disagreement.

He scooted off the table, taking half of the tissue paper with him. "This protection is nonsensical. You'd think by now they would make something more practical."

As he dressed back into his pressed black slacks and pale-blue Oxford button-down, Alexander contemplated leaving the library in someone else's hands. It would be disastrous at the very least. There was no one else in town qualified to run the library.

The pain stretched vertically in his back as he slipped on his dress shoes. While he had no choice with regards to the surgery, he would do everything in his power to devise a plan for the library in his short absence. Even if doing so meant canceling the Library's Christmas Celebration for the first time in history.

The sleigh bells attached to the door jingled as Alexander entered Breakfast, Lunch, Dinner & Everything in Between to pick up his to-go order on the way home from the doctor's appointment in Cactus City. Usually, he would stay to eat, but his back was hurting yet again, and the last thing he wanted to do was sit on a ridged chair or a worn vinyl bench.

"Alexander!" Lillian called from behind the bar's counter. "I just finished making your dinner. Let me wrap it up for you." She hurried around the corner, through the swinging doors, and into the kitchen.

Even though Alexander was considerably particular about what he ate, Lillian could make anything and he would undoubtedly enjoy it. Unlike his father's fare. William, whose vision grew worse by the day, refused to stop cooking. Alexander tried to distract his dad from the kitchen, not only for William's physical safety, but also for his own stomach's safety. His father might have been a great cook back in the day, but with his poor eyesight paired with zero sense of smell, he often confused his spices. To William, ground clove was the same as ground pepper.

"Alexander, great seeing you. Did you hear April's back in town?" Luis approached the front of the restaurant with several menus in hand.

"April," he paused. "Yes, April—your old waitress."

"She's your age. You two graduated high school together, so I don't think of her as old, but anyhoo, yes, April."

"Good news indeed," Alexander smiled, although he was unsure what the big deal was. April was not born and raised in Woolsey, she only went to high school here, and it was noticeable when she kept saying *Prescott* incorrectly. Non-natives didn't know Prescott was pronounced with an *i* sound where the *o* was.

"She's already dived back into running the *Woolsey Times*," Luis added. "Come to think of it, April might be the perfect match."

"Perfect match?" *What was Luis getting at?*

Sure, Alexander would never admit to anyone other than himself that he found April attractive. Not that that meant anything. They hadn't chatted much in high school, seeing as though they were complete opposites and mere acquaintances who ran into each other around town off and on until she finally left for college.

April had been the most popular girl in school, and he had been the least. She was only two months older than him, but she took her time pursuing a degree—too long, in his opinion. She could've gone to college and been well on her way to a long-standing career if she hadn't spent years waitressing at the diner. He only knew when her birthday was because everyone at school made such a big deal about it, not because he cared to remember for his own sake.

He couldn't recall the last time he'd seen April, but if she was as beautiful as he remembered, she would have a boyfriend, if not a fiancé. He was sure Luis meant something else with his matchmaking comment.

"Yes, the perfect person to cover for you at the library," Luis finally finished.

"I see." Alexander straightened his posture, grateful his little high school secret remained hidden. "I don't believe I'll be out long enough, contrary to what the doctor assumes. I've always been a fast healer. Besides, it would be best—if there were a need for coverage—for the individual to have library experience."

"That's what's perfect about April. Her degree is in library science." Luis patted Alexander on the side of his arm. "A friend of mine out in Phoenix had back surgery, and he was out much longer than expected."

Before Alexander could retort, Lillian appeared with a sandwich-size box and a foil-wrapped item on top. Inside would be his four-cheese ravioli and garlic bread. His mouth watered thinking about how delightful it would taste.

"Here ya go," Lillian said as she handed it over.

"Thank you." He removed his credit card from his wallet and handed it to Luis, who promptly hurried off to swipe it.

"You really ought to think about April being your replacement," Luis said as he handed the credit card back. "The entire town always looks forward to the Christmas celebration there, and we'd hate for it to be canceled this year."

"I'll keep that in mind." Alexander offered a smile and then turned toward the door. "Have a good evening. And don't fret about the LCC, it will go off without a hitch."

Alexander climbed into his car, set his meal on the passenger seat, and started the engine. The chill outside caused him to rub his hands together as the air from the vents began to warm. The sun had set behind the mountains and with it, the little bit of heat it provided disappeared. It was the end of November, and the temperatures had fully given way to fall. It was hard for anyone, even a Woolsey resident, to go from one hundred and twenty to fifty degrees and not have the body feel some sort of shock.

He backed out of the parking spot and turned onto State Route 287. Alexander hadn't used the heater since February, and the scent of burning dust filtered around the vehicle, forcing him to crack the window, allowing it to escape.

Being cold was not good for his back muscles, and thankfully, his house was a short drive. He halted at the stop sign, then turned left on the road that led to the school, city center, and just before those, the two-acre parcel of land he shared with his father.

His house was front and center, a respectable mobile home built slightly off the ground on a concrete slab. William occupied the smaller mobile home to the right, and while it was an older model, it was still a nice trailer.

He knew trailer homes got a much worse rap than they deserved. Of course Alexander planned to build a tiny home someday and have the trailer hauled away, but librarians didn't make much—especially in a town as small as Woolsey.

Both trailers' front porch lights were on, allowing him to see better through the dust that crept across the dry landscape. After parking in front of his home, Alexander made his way to his dad's place and gave a quick knock on the door before opening it. His father was careless about remembering to lock his door. He'd grown up in Woolsey, back when there was no school, no grocery store, and no diner—a different time.

"Hi, Dad. I thought I told you to keep the door locked." Alexander stood in the small linoleum-covered entry-way.

William sat in his cobalt-blue recliner with a mug of tea steaming on the TV tray he used as a side table and lifted the remote at the television to mute it. The trailer was clean but small and just the right size for a man of his father's age—the less to keep tidy, the better.

His dad shifted in his chair and motioned with his hand. "It's fine. I have nothing to steal."

"That's not what I'm worried about." Alexander inspected the area without moving. "Did you eat dinner and take your medications?"

"Of course. My vision is going, not my mind."

"You decorated already?" Alexander pointed at the tabletop Christmas tree and garland strung around the TV's 1990s entertainment center.

"Yes, it's after Thanksgiving. Not all of us are bah humbugs."

"I'm no such thing. I decorate."

"Ah, yes, I know, my son. Precisely on December 1, and only the bare minimal."

Alexander waved his right hand in the air. "It's not as though you go all out yourself, Dad."

"I'm not young like you. If I put up a full-size tree, I'd throw out my hip and back in one go."

"My upcoming back surgery begs to differ with you that age has anything to do with it." Alexander opened the door and stepped back outside. "Good night, Dad."

"Good night, son."

Before heading to his trailer, Alexander slipped his copy of the house key into his father's lock, and secured his front door.

As he stopped at his car to grab the food, he spotted a light coming on in the house across the way. April's parents' home. He couldn't help but think about her return as the pain in his back niggled at him. Maybe he would have to see if she was available to run the library for a day. Two days, maximum.

Chapter 2

April

April Gardner had no idea what to do now that she was back in Woolsey. But she was grateful that her parents, now retired, had finally taken up residence in their RV to travel the country together—a lifelong plan of theirs.

She only had one month before her parents returned and took back their home. And sadly, even with her degree in hand, she knew there was nothing in Woolsey for her to do. She could've stayed in the bustling city—thanks to Frank, her therapy dog—but she missed home and didn't have a job to keep her in Seattle any longer. Sure, she'd already jumped back into managing the town's newspaper, but the pay meant it was more of a hobby than a job.

There was the library, but there was only room for one librarian in town, and that job belonged to the ridged-as-a-book's-spine Alexander. And he'd probably work there until the day he died. They'd been classmates in high school but never got around to being friends, even though there weren't a lot of choices to pick from.

She and Alexander couldn't be more opposite in all the ways life had to offer. She learned through their mutual classes that they didn't like the same music or books. At lunchtime, April knew they didn't like the same foods, and during assemblies her mind daydreamed while he studied everything around him as though preparing for a test. He was probably one of those people who made their bed in the morning even though no one came over to see it and it would only get messed up again come bedtime.

April made her way from the kitchen into the living room when she sneezed. Frank, her tan-and-white bulldog, who'd been asleep on the couch, jumped nearly a foot in the air. And then she sneezed again.

"Sorry, buddy." She yanked another tissue from the holder and sneezed into it. Her eyes watered as her cell phone vibrated on the kitchen island. Through filtered vision, she hurried to it.

"Hallo?"

"You sound like your head's going to explode out your nose," Trinity's voice came through the line, "but I'm glad you're back to running the paper. It was sort of a mess with Jennifer in charge while you were gone. Anyways, I wanted to see if you still had any ad space for December's edition?"

"Yes, I can squeeze that in before the deadline. Do you—achoo—want to run another spot for your cookies?" April pinched her eyes close as they filled with tears, her sinuses burning.

"Yes, I want to run a Christmas special. I'll email you the graphic. Just bill my account."

April held her breath as though doing so would avert the sneeze.

"How have you been?" Trinity cleared her throat.

"I'm glad to be back. Washington's weather was wearing on me."

"I'm sure your parents are grateful you can keep up the house while they're gone. Shoot, I'd better go. My mom has a late shift at the restaurant, and for every minute I'm late, she gives Jolie a piece of candy. I told her to take her to work, that Luis won't mind, and I can pick her up there. But I think she has more fun hearing about Jolie bouncing off the walls from her deliberately induced sugar rush. Thanks again, April. I'll get that email over to you."

April sneezed. "You're welcome."

"You should get a shot for that."

"A shot?" She blew loudly into her tissue.

"Yes. A shot for allergies."

April sniffed. "I don't do well with shots. If I did, I'd have become a nurse. I was going to see if Charlie carried something over at the store."

"Best of luck. I have a great one—Stop Sneeze. I've been using it for a few months now."

"Sounds perfect."

"Got it in Cactus City," Trinity sighed. "And I'm out of my stash. Maybe Charlie carries it now?"

April held up her fingers, crossing her pointer over her middle finger. "Let's hope."

Then she pressed her finger to her nose like a fake mustache. "I'm going to go before I sneeze again."

After stopping by Shop and Save, and leaving with everything but the allergy medicine, April entered her parents' home through the garage door to find Frank had gotten into a bit of trouble.

April heaved the paper bag of groceries onto the countertop nearest her. "Frank." She placed hands on her hips. "What happened?"

The bulldog lifted his head, pushed himself up off the pile of magazines he'd shredded, and trotted over to her. His blocky face wedged between her ankles. She bent down to rub the wrinkles on his face when she sneezed and nearly lost her balance.

"Hopefully Grandma didn't want to read these. We're lucky she loves you and thinks you can't ever do anything wrong." April went to her knees and began to collect the glossy destroyed pages. Frank flopped down and attempted to roll onto his back. "Yes, of course you make me happy, too." She sneezed, and her hair caught in her mouth at the corner.

Actually, Frank did more than make her happy; he'd saved her in college and made completing her degree possible. At times, she'd worried that waiting so long to leave Woolsey was because she was more afraid of change than she imagined. Anxiety was not something April dealt with regularly growing up, but upon arriving in Seattle, she'd become instantly overwhelmed by the busyness of the city. Finding herself afraid to leave her dorm room, she spoke with the school's counselor, who'd suggested a therapy dog. Of course, that meant people would most likely make nasty, rude comments under their breath about them. But with Frank, she'd been able to stay in the city and not return home as a failure.

At first, she'd scolded herself for thinking something like that wouldn't happen to her, coming from Woolsey. Even though April had been born outside of Woolsey, she'd always lived in a town with a population of the community college on a slow day. And it wasn't until she moved away for college that she realized she had an unknown problem.

Frank had been a lifesaver, keeping her off medication and making it possible to complete her degree. As time went on, and students and faculty became more aware, things changed. When they saw Frank and her coming their way, they would either give them more space or approach them with a welcoming smile, wanting to say hi to the bulldog. Yet even being in Seattle for four years, April never got used to life there and knew that any career path she chose would need to be in a small town or someplace that allowed Frank to be with her.

After heating up some hot cocoa in the microwave, April dropped an overflowing handful of mini marshmallows into the snowman mug. Then she opened the back slider, allowing the sixty-degree breeze to waft into the living room.

She located *Just Friends*, a Christmas movie most people forget about during the holidays, on the TV and swiped the first coat of Santa Red onto her toenails which rested on the edge of the coffee table.

Her parents' house hadn't changed in all the years they'd lived here. The couch was as old as she was, its blue-and-peach-colored stripes straight out of a '90s Florida décor magazine. Thankfully, her parents had updated their TV. Though it had been purchased a few years ago and some would already classify it as outdated, it was far better than the one they'd had with the built-in VHS player. But the place was cozy, and she didn't want to leave. Sadly, she also couldn't stay forever, no matter how much she loved Woolsey. April needed to make her own life someplace that welcomed Frank.

But this holiday would be less magical than any other ones since her parents would be spending it in New York. They'd invited her to fly up with Frank and visit them, but to be honest, even with Frank, New York City sounded as scary as scary could be.

She sighed and stood up, walking with her toes up in the air to keep them from smudging. The breeze was gentle and cool on her cheeks as she pulled the screen door open and stepped onto the back patio. Tonight, like most nights, the sky was without a cloud, and the stars were enhanced by the midnight blue.

April took a nearby patio chair and dragged it to the edge of the patio covering as she sneezed twice in a row.

She carefully walked around to the front of it and sat down. Frank had waddled out behind her and flopped onto his raised dog bed nearby. Resting her head on the back of the chair, she stared up at the stars, making a Christmas wish that whatever happened in December would provide all the answers she needed on what to do next.

After finishing her wish, a light directly to her left caught her vision. The only two-story home in all of Woolsey was Aurora Easton's. And one didn't need to live across the street from Aurora to see the light come on in town. But that was not all she saw—the house had already been decorated for Christmas. The only homes in Woolsey without holiday decorations were her parents' and Alexander's. She didn't even need to drive by his trailer to know that. William had his lights up—as he had them up 365 days a year, but he only turned them on from Thanksgiving to New Year's Day and for the entire month of July because he fully believed in "Christmas in July."

Regardless of anyone's opinion on the July display, they were too much work for the seventy-seven-year-old man to be stringing them up and taking them down every holiday season. And April vowed that Alexander would be the only humbug of Woolsey by sunset tomorrow night.

Snatching the tissue from her pocket, April blew her nose while gazing at the soft glow illuminating Alexander's windows. No matter how much she didn't want to bother him, she also knew he might be her only hope if

16

she wanted to get some peace. "Hopefully, I don't look too miserable."

April glanced over at Frank, who appeared to have become one with the dog bed, his prominent overbite the only visible thing in the dark of the night. If a bartender got a look at Frank, he would've cut him off hours ago if he were human.

She sneezed again, grabbing ahold of the chair's arm. "Okay, I'm going to walk over there and ask. It's not like he doesn't know me. Just because we haven't talked to each other and don't exactly have a friendship doesn't mean I can't stop by. Alexander is still Alexander, and I'm still me." *And he's still handsome.*

April took her mug to the kitchen and located her cheap flip-flops by the front door while Frank continued lounging. When she returned to the patio, she told him, "Let's go for a walk."

The bulldog lifted his head and lowered it before deciding to stand and stretch. Being with her, even if it meant walking, was far better than being lazy and alone.

Chapter 3

Alexander

Alexander had just made himself a double peanut butter hot chocolate and set it on the cork coaster next to the latest novel he was reading when his doorbell chimed. On his way to answer it, he passed by his Persian ginger tabby, Cora, curled up on the top of his couch and gave her a quick pet.

When he opened the door, the last person he expected to see was her.

"Good evening, April, I heard you were back in town."

"Hallo, yes, I'm back. Please, please"—April grasped her hands together while he watched her dog sniff around the clay pot of purple and yellow pansies wedged into the corner next to the door—"tell me you have Stop Sneeze. I stopped by the store, but Charlie had no idea what I was talking about." She held a finger to her nose. "I'm going to die from these allergies."

"That would be a first." Alexander crossed his arms as the chill of night air crept over him. "Dying from allergies, I don't think that's possible."

April held up her finger and looked as though she was about to respond when she sneezed three times, her shoulder-length espresso hair whipping forward.

Even when her cheeks and nose were shades of pink, Alexander found himself caught off guard by April's beauty. The way her eyes picked up the light and her soft smile seemed utterly natural, as though she didn't have to force it upon her lips, she simply exuded happiness from within.

"Please." She reached her hand out and pressed it against his chest. The warmth of her palm through his shirt diverted his eyes from her lips to his chest.

"Sorry." April pulled her hand back.

"The good news is I do have some of that Stop Sneeze medication. I'll get you a few pills." He turned and sauntered into the kitchen.

Alexander knew that the flush traveling up his neck was not from the warmth of his trailer's heater. He couldn't deny he'd thought about her off and on since she left for college. However, he didn't expect April to return and for him still have those hidden feelings of affection towards her.

He went to his bathroom, poured three Stop Sneeze pills into a small container, and returned to the open front door to find April's back to him. He shook the bottle to get her attention. And when she spun around, he saw she'd shoved a tissue up her nose.

"I've heard the Museum of Natural History is looking for the elusive Tissue Mammoth." He paused at the threshold. Even with a tissue hanging from her nose, she was cute.

"Alexander has jokes?" She pressed her hand to her nose, and the tissue went with it when she pulled away. "Thank you so much. I feel like I'm ten minutes from cutting off the front of my face."

He gave a huff of a laugh and handed her the container. "You always were a bit dramatic."

Their fingertips brushed when she took the container from him, and he wondered if it sent tingles up her hand like it had his.

"If you felt like I do, you would understand I'm not even close to being dramatic." April popped off the lid, placed one of the white oval pills into her mouth, and swallowed, patting her neck. "As soon as I can drive without my eyes watering, I'm heading to Cactus City to stock up, *if* these work."

Alexander shifted on his feet and glanced back at the kitchen. "I can't believe you swallowed that without water. Can I ... Do you ...?"

She sneezed.

"Do you need water?" He opened the door farther and moved out of the way, forgetting that Frank was standing next to her.

"Frank is not a fan of cats." She pointed at Cora. "Maybe another time when my head doesn't feel like it's going to blow off my face."

"You have a way with words. And I believe Frank would be a good boy around Cora." Alexander pointed at the dog. "He doesn't strike me as able to jump high enough to reach her."

"He might surprise you. Frank saved me at college." April glanced down at him and then pivoted on the heels of her boots. "My nose thanks you," she called over her shoulder and stepped down into the driveway.

"You're welcome." He watched her walk back toward her parents' home, crossing over the small wash with Frank close to her heels.

Folding his arm across his body, he kept his vision on April until her silhouette faded and the glow of the house lights was disturbed. But her words stuck in his mind. What did she mean by Frank saved her?

As he turned to head back inside, something dropped from above the door frame and sent Alexander stumbling backward.

On his welcome mat, a snake, about two feet long, slithering to the right of his shoe.

"Crap!" He leapt back, his hand went to his tailbone. The sudden jerk of his body caused his back pain to radiate. "Cora!" Alexander called as though his cat were a dog and would come to assist with chasing the snake away. "Cora!"

He eyed the snake pressed up against where the decking paired with the trailer's siding. The snake's scales varied in color beginning with a darkened head that lightened further down its body, which meant it was a Coachwhip and not a rattler.

But he still wanted the snake to know his cat would happily chase him far from the house. "Cora!"

Alexander stomped his shoe on the deck as the Coachwhip lived up to its name. It whipped its tail with a snap and jetted away from the siding and off the porch. Cora popped her head around the front door, spotting the snake in the dirt at the bottom of the steps. If she didn't catch it, at least she'd be entertained chasing it around.

He had no idea why the Coachwhip was even here. Usually, snakes went into hibernation by the end of October. As he calmed his nerves, he glanced over at April's parents' house again and studied it as the moon's light reflected off the back windows. Even with the startle of a snake, his thoughts went to her. She was everything he wasn't, and somehow it caused his heart to flutter.

Chapter 4

April

Throughout the night, the sound of raspy snuffled-up-blubber gasps echoed off the bedroom walls from both her and Frank. So, early in the morning, as April rubbed her eyes and sat up in bed, she took a deep breath through her nose with delight to breathe again. Although it took a while, the Stop Sneeze had worked. She snatched her phone off the nightstand to check the time and realized it didn't matter. Yet another day that April had no place to be.

"Frank! Frankster! Frankie! Frankoreno!" She rubbed his belly as he lay next to her, sprawled out. "Let's go get breakfast. I bet it's even cool enough to cozy up on the back patio with a sweater."

April climbed from the bed, leaving Frank to think about if he wanted to get up or go back to sleep.

Her bare feet padded over the cold tile, and she snatched the eggplant-colored fuzzy sweater off the back of the couch as she headed into the kitchen. While preparing the coffee, her vision was drawn toward the

23

kitchen's window. Why was she thinking about Alexander? She'd been home for only a few days, and he hadn't even crossed her mind until she saw him yesterday evening. Sure, he was handsome, but not her type, and she wasn't staying in town for long even if he were.

While the coffee dripped, she approached the stack of novels on the coffee table and spread them out like a deck of cards in a magic trick. She brought her hand over her eyes and pointed with her other.

"Eeny, meenie, miney, moe."

April opened her eyes to find her finger on a hardcover book.

"Oh, this one looks good but heavy . . ." She lifted the book off the table and cradled it to her chest. The scent of the ancient paper and ink tickled her nose with delight.

She gripped the coffee pot and poured it into a white mug covered with evergreen trees and headed outside to the patio's worn wooden rocking chair. Setting the mug on the glass-topped side table, April eased into the chair and took a deep breath. The scent of wild grasses in the air caused her to nearly sneeze. But the medication Alexander had given her was working, and she thought this might be the first time in years she could actually smell the late November air.

April looked out at the landscape. The Arizona ash trees had started to turn golden as they danced in the breeze. By January, the bitterbrush blanketing the desert would be in bloom with its bright-yellow flowers. She'd missed the view and weather more than she'd realized.

The peacefulness of not having to deal with the sensory overload of Seattle was a nice break.

She took a sip of her hot coffee, flavored with hazelnut crème, and opened the book. Easing back into the chair, Frank waddled out the slider and onto the patio. Bees buzzed in the pink and white pansies blooming in the aqua-blue pots flanking the back patio under the lattice awning.

April paused and smiled, grateful that she could sit outside thanks to Alexander. She leaned forward and set her coffee mug on the table and returned to the book when something dark fell directly in front of her vision and landed in the crease where the pages met.

A scream loud enough to be heard in Cactus City vibrated from April's mouth. A scorpion had fallen from the awning and landed in her book. When she sprang up from the chair, she heaved the open book forward and watched it fly across the patio.

When it landed, a plume of dust kicked up. April rubbed her hands over her body to check that no other scorpions were crawling on her. Her fingers weaved into her hair, and she frantically shook her head.

Frank hurried to April and turned, sitting on top of her feet. As April peered over at the book, which had closed from the force of the drop, she caught Alexander speed walking toward the backyard.

"Are you alright?" he called out once he reached the other side of the wash.

"Be careful. There's a scorpion . . . someplace over there." April continued to rub her hands on her arms, checking that nothing else was crawling on her.

"What happened?" Alexander paused in front of the thrown book. He wore dark pants, Chelsea boots, and an ironed In Memory of Granite Mountain Hotshots T-shirt.

"A scorpion dropped from"—she motioned to the rocking chair—"I guess the awning . . . onto my book."

"Oh." He bent down, resting his forearms on the top of his legs, and observed the book lying closed in the dirt. "I hate when that happens. When they transition from area to area, they never seem to make it too far. Do you think the scorpion is under the book?"

"I sure hope so."

"*Bleak House*. I'm surprised you're reading that book." He glanced up at her, and she placed a hand on top of her head. For some reason, she didn't expect Alexander to be the nature type. He was always reserved in school, with his face behind a book and far from anything nature-like that would dirty his clothes. "Would you please bring me a stick or something long?"

She hurried inside and snatched the broom off the hanger in the kitchen pantry. When April handed it over to Alexander, she stretched her arm out, keeping her distance from the book.

"Why does my choice of books surprise you?" She wrapped herself up in her sweater.

He looked up at April, squinting against the morning sunshine. "I take you as more of an *Anne of Green Gables*, *Little Woman* type. Classic women's fiction."

"I'm more of a Gaskell or Fitzgerald type."

"I think you squished it." Alexander took the broom handle and used it to push the book away. "Yes, he's a goner."

April stepped a foot closer. "If Mr. Dickens didn't write such lengthy books, he might have had a chance."

"A romance novel would've saved him for sure." Alexander stood up straight and hinted at a smile.

"I'm not a big fan of romance novels."

"Because?"

She crossed her arms as Frank trotted over to greet Alexander. "*Because* they're . . . I guess I find love to be a challenge, and they always make it look effortless."

"I might be inclined to agree."

"So you read romance novels?" April shivered as Alexander pushed the book away from the deceased scorpion before picking it up.

"No." His voice went up an octave as he drew out the *o*.

April took the book as he handed it over, and she brushed off the dirt. Questions swirled in her mind like a dust devil. She craved to find out what romance novels he'd read and wondered what else she didn't know about him.

"I think I owe some patrons an apology." He pointed at the book. "Reading can kill you."

April let out a snort-laugh and covered her mouth to try and hide her embarrassment.

"The allergy medicine seems like it's working." He pointed in the direction of her nose.

"Yes." She pulled the book close to her chest, realizing she was in her pajamas, hoping the novel would at least cover a few square inches. "Thank you. I'm going to head into Cactus City today, pick up some, and restock your supply."

"You looked miserable last night." He shoved his left hand in his front pocket. "Not ugly, miserable. You looked allergy miserable. You still looked like you."

Oh my goodness, he's nervous. Wait, why is he nervous?

"Do you have something with which I can scoop up the scorpion?"

"I'll grab the dustpan." April took two steps backward before spinning around. She knew she should feel bad about killing a living thing, but the scorpion could've easily bitten her or Frank, which was a risk she would never take.

As she collected the dustpan, she thought of how quickly Alexander had come to her rescue. The notion caused her to check her reflection in the microwave door before going back outside. And as she exited onto the patio, she knew her life was turning into a romance novel, and she would have to stop it.

28

Chapter 5

Alexander

After propping open the library's door, Alexander adjusted his crimson tie. He grabbed a pair of scissors and cut open the small box that rested on the library's checkout desk. Two new hardback books had come in, and he inhaled a quick sniff of them, appreciating the scent of fresh paper and ink that filled his nose.

"Are you sniffing a book?" a female voice startled him.

He swung the book away from his face. "April." Alexander looked down at the floor. "And Frank."

"Oh, I didn't mean to startle you." April, dressed in a green-and-red floral cocktail dress, clutched her purse over her shoulder, Frank's leash, and a plastic bag in the other hand. "I hope it's okay that Frank is with me. Being a therapy dog, he should be allowed in here."

He wasn't surprised to see her. First of all, she owed him three Stop Sneeze pills, and second, it'd been twenty-four hours since Luis proposed the idea—long enough for the news to have spread through town that he was going to be out for surgery and April would be his perfect replacement.

"Yes, rules are rules, and we allow for service animals." Of course, he wanted to find out why she now had a therapy dog when she didn't have one in high school and displayed no obvious cause for needing one.

"Can you believe how cold it is outside?" She removed her plum-colored gloves like she was in a 1950s movie, pinching the tips.

"Forty-three degrees is a might chilly." Alexander remained behind the desk.

Today, April had soft curls framing her heart-shaped face. He drew his hand to his chin, hoping he'd had a close enough shave this morning. Unfortunately, she'd interrupted his morning routine with her death scream over the scorpion. And by the time he returned home, Alexander had been somewhat flustered and rushed through the rest of his morning routine.

"I thought I might have to turn the heater on last night, but the second cup of hot cocoa warmed me up nicely." She gazed around the library. "You haven't decorated for Christmas yet?"

"It's not December 1." He set the book down and walked around the desk.

He'd never realized they were the same height before, and Alexander took a quick peek to see if she was wearing heels. When he spotted her three-inch boots, he sighed inside, thankful he was not shrinking due to his back issues. At his young age, that would put him in a pickle.

"You know, there is no law that says you can't decorate for Christmas *before* December 1." She smiled, and it warmed him all the way to his toes, and for a brief second, he wanted to snatch the box of holiday decor and decorate early. Then he pulled himself from such a convoluted notion when a sharp pain lanced across his lower back.

"Where is the point of your tie?" April motioned with her red nails.

He glanced down, one hand rubbing at the pain in his back. "What do you mean?"

She moved closer and took hold of his tie in her hand, running her fingers midway to the end. "It's a flat-bottom tie. I don't think I've seen that before—or if I have, I've forgotten about it."

Alexander took hold of the end of his tie from April. "Yes, it reminds me of a bookmark." He flicked the end between his fingers. When he glanced up, she'd not stepped back, and the color of her eyes reminded him of honey.

"I should probably get to why I'm here."

"Stop Sneeze," he reminded her.

April stretched out her arm and handed over the plastic bag. "I guess two things, then."

He pressed his eyes closed for a second and then said, "How about a new library card?"

"Nice try. I know, you know."

"I do." Alexander stepped around her and back to his desk. "It's temporary and only two days maximum.

My surgery is scheduled for Friday, when we're closed. Therefore, I'll only need you for Saturday."

"Are you sure you should be back at work that early? I thought you'd be out for at least a week."

"I'm a fast healer. And regardless, I'll need to set up for the library's annual Christmas festivities."

"I'm delighted you still do that, and I'm sure the town is, too."

"The Library's Christmas Celebration." Alexander adjusted a stack of books so they all lined up perfectly. "Traditions must be upheld."

"Well, aren't you just the joy of the holiday season?" She waved him off and spun around, the bottom of her dress flaring out slightly. "So, where should I start?"

"There should be a formal interview. Don't you suppose?" He eased his hands into the front pockets of his pants.

April placed her left hand over her mouth and giggled. "An interview? Alexander, you must be joking."

"That would be the proper way to handle it. You'll receive a paycheck, and I'm not aware of anyone who works that hasn't required an interview."

April walked over to a nearby study table and pulled out the chair. Frank waddled after her and flopped down at her feet. She folded her hands together and rested them atop the cherry-stained wood. "Okay, I'm ready for my interview."

Alexander removed his hands from his pockets and glanced around the library as though he might find someone else to handle the interview.

"Well, you don't expect me to interview myself, do you?" April wiggled in the chair, bringing her posture straight.

He stepped forward and stood behind the chair opposite of her. "I must mention, I've never interviewed anyone before and, frankly, don't know what to ask."

"My qualifications are as follows. I have my bachelor's degree in library science and have completed an internship at the university's library for three months as part of my requirements. While I was not born in Woolsey, as you recall, I attended the local high school from freshman year to graduation and remained in town, working at the restaurant for several years before leaving for college."

"And Frank. I see he has a service vest." Alexander glanced around the top of the table.

"Yes, rather embarrassing, but it turns out living in Woolsey conditioned me for quiet and calm and moving to Seattle caused a bit of anxiety. Let's just say I'm glad I didn't try to go to college in Los Angeles."

Alexander gripped the top of the chair. "Do you have agoraphobia?"

"Not quite. I have a fear of large objects—towering buildings, cruise ships, even oversize crowds—but not leaving the house. The psychiatrist referred to it as more of megalophobia. As you can imagine, being on a large university campus was not ideal."

"Couldn't you have gotten your degree online?"

"Not all of it. I needed to complete an internship, and while I did take some classes online when I first arrived, it was Frank that made it possible to attend in-person classes and thus graduate."

He found himself staring at April, thinking about everything she said. He had no idea what it must have been like to have those fears, unknown until she moved away, and then need to face them quickly. But, even with the help of Frank, he knew she'd had to be strong enough on her own to take the first steps.

"So, do I have the job?" April stood up.

Alexander had fears also. Fears of someone else running the library and running it incorrectly. Not to mention, messing up everything he'd worked for and perfected. "I suppose for this weekend. We're open from twelve to three on Saturday and Sunday."

"What about Monday?"

"We're open from eight to four, but I'll be back by Monday."

April rocked on her heels and tapped the right one. "Don't worry about a thing. I'll have everything under control." She turned her head and smiled, gazing around at the library.

He was indeed worried, but instead of letting her know, he smiled, too.

Chapter 6

April

That was the worst fake smile April had seen since her roommate in college tried to hide the fact that she was okay with failing her thesis report.

"He obviously doesn't trust me with his library," April said to Frank while he sat in the passenger seat, as she pulled into the parking lot of Shop and Save.

Bold-colored Christmas lights wrapped around the posts that supported the awning of the linear patio. Soft white twinkling lights were strung around the windows and main door, and *Merry Christmas* window clings were plastered about. The smoker and barbecue were off to the side and covered for the winter season. One would be hard-pressed to find Woolsey residents sitting out in the cold this time of year.

April's parents had left her with only a casserole that appeared to be a few days old and condiments in the refrigerator. After a dinner of double hot chocolate last night, her blood sugar levels couldn't take it again.

The warmth of the store, mixed with the scent of cinnamon and sugar, greeted her as she entered.

"April!"

She turned to her right to see Aurora and her daughters, Willa and Ava, dressed in Christmas sweaters.

"Hi, it's so great to see you." April gave Aurora a quick hug then lowered herself to the little girls' level. "I love your sweaters."

Ava reached her hand out toward Frank, and the bulldog sniffed it. "I love your dog."

"Frank says thank you." April pet the top of his head before standing back up.

"We just came in to grab a few things for our road trip to Prescott. It snowed the other night, so we figured let's make the most of it and do our Christmas photo." Aurora glanced around. "Gavin is here someplace." She placed her hand near her mouth to block her daughter from seeing her lips. "Probably looking to see if Charlie has any leftover gosh-awful candy corn."

April nodded in agreement. "Not a fan of that stuff myself. I heard your nonprofit is shaping up nicely. That's so great." April grabbed a cart and used it to lean on. Her heeled shoes worked great outside of Woolsey—she hadn't done much walking in the dirt in Seattle—but now she needed to remember where she was.

"Thank you. Gavin was a great help getting the windmills built."

"Tell him I said hi, and have a safe drive. It's always crazy with traffic when it snows so close to Phoenix."

Aurora stepped forward, and they hugged goodbye.

"Oh," April said. "Trinity's cookies, the eggless ones, Charlie still sells them, right? I didn't see them in my allergy-induced fog yesterday."

Aurora pointed near the checkout lane. "Yes, I think they're on the end cap at the register line. And she has a new holiday one out, too."

"I'll have to get those. I thought I'd packed enough when I left last time, but I was sorely mistaken."

Aurora smiled as Ava tugged on April's hand. "Can I pet Frank goodbye?"

"Yes, thank you for asking."

Ava bent at the waist, gave the bulldog a few rubs on the head, and then waved. "Bye, Frank."

As the Easton girls headed off to find Gavin, April motioned for Frank to follow her further into the store.

Every end cap was stuffed full of treats—from candy canes to chocolate Christmas bells. Her stomach grumbled as she reached for a few bags and tossed them into the cart. She took her time strolling through the store. It was nice not having to deal with crowds and wait for people to get out of the way so she could grab something off the shelf. The nearest grocery store to the university was open 24-7 and busy every one of those hours. Even with Frank's help, she'd decided it was too much and usually had groceries delivered.

As April rounded the corner, she spotted William, Alexander's father, at the deli counter.

"Are you ordering the library's holiday ham?" April asked.

William turned around, and his face lit up like a Christmas star on top of a tree. "Little April."

He'd always called her that, even after she no longer could be classified as little. It started back when she moved to Woolsey, and although she'd been a freshman in high school, she'd been the shortest one, and his son, Alex, a close second.

"Hi, Mr. Adams. It's wonderful to see you." She moved to hug him. "How have you been doing?"

"My old knees are getting older, and my old vision is much worse. Do yourself a favor—stop aging."

April laughed. "Well, I'll see what I can do. Besides, Mr. Adams, I think at this point in life you're entitled to a few aches and pains." April adjusted her scarf. "Are you still in charge of the cacti lighting?"

"Absolutely. I hope you'll be there this year."

It was a Woolsey Christmas tradition to decorate the five massive saguaro cacti in the middle of the city center's parking lot. Towns worldwide had tree lightings, but in Woolsey, Arizona, it was cacti lighting.

However unique and quirky it was, decorating cacti with lights was a chore for whoever was stuck with the task. They had to be careful to maintain the integrity of the saguaro since they were an endangered plant in Arizona. Preparing them for the lighting took about five hours, and April knew this because each year she'd drive by in the morning, and by lunch, they'd finally be wrapping up.

"I wouldn't miss it." She smiled. "What else are you up to these days?"

"R. J. has been teaching me wood carving. And Sydney over at the post office is teaching me how to knit. But both are testing me, with my eyesight getting worse every week, it seems. They agree I can do both without adequate vision just by knowing the rhythm of the hooks and feeling the wood. I guess since I can't really see the outcome that's correct. However, I've been watching that YouTube—a fine thing—and I'm learning to cook like some of the shows the best I can. A man can only take so many ham sandwiches with a side of beans."

"I'll take your word for it."

April had noticed how much Alexander resembled his father in the looks department, but their personalities were vastly different. She could actually stand being around William. He was the opposite of his strict son, and she wondered what happened that caused Alexander to be a complete nincompoop.

"Thank you for stepping in to help over at the library while my son recuperates. Hopefully, he won't be out too long." He peeked over the deli case.

"You've already heard? I'm surprised because Alexander didn't seem like he wanted to ask me in the first place."

"Alexander didn't inform me about it, and you're correct, he didn't want to ask you or anyone. You know how he can be. Charlie told me, who heard it from Trinity, who heard it from Lillian, who saw you leaving the library."

"Well, maybe if you get the word out that you need some help picking out your ham, it might be faster than waiting for the butcher," April said.

"Good idea." He wagged his finger at her.

"Sorry," a voice called out as the door swung open behind the deli case. "Here ya go, William." Lucas, the butcher, carried something large and dropped it on the counter in front of him with a thump. "I have your ham."

"Wow, that's mighty . . . big," April exclaimed and leaned forward at the same time Mr. Adams did. "How many people are going to the library celebration? Did we invite all of Cactus City, too?"

William continued to lean forward as though he were examining a body at a crime scene. "I ordered it early, to be safe. Maybe I wrote down the wrong size on the form. I struggle with seeing print."

"Need some help putting this in your cart, William?" Lucas asked, looking at it but not picking it back up.

"If you don't mind, thanks," Mr. Adams said, pushing his cart to the side of the deli case.

"Short Stuff Gardner, I heard you were back in town."

"Hi, Lucas." She nodded. They'd dated so long ago—their entire sophomore year in high school—but her nickname never disappeared from his lips. She didn't mind being called Short Stuff, but she preferred April. Short Stuff made her feel like she was a stuffed turkey.

April nodded her head. "Yes, yes, I am. I'm in town."

"If you're free, we could grab dinner over at the diner later?" Lucas asked as Mr. Adams's eyes shifted between them both.

"I'll have to take a rain check. Trying to get settled back into the rhythm, and I don't know how keen Luis would be with Frank coming in." She glanced down at the bulldog sitting next to her heels on the linoleum and wiggled his leash.

"A dog?" Lucas lifted the ham, carried it around the counter, and set it in Mr. Adams's cart. "Here you go, William. I hope I get to try a slice."

"That's the plan. Thank you, I'd best get going. Lots to do." The old man hurried off as fast as his tired legs could muster.

"A service dog for Short Stuff?" Lucas crossed his arms over his dirty white apron, but his gorgeous Nordic-blue eyes questioned Frank's presence. "I will hold you to the rain check, Short Stuff."

"It's April or Ms. Gardner. Either works, thanks. Great seeing you, Lucas." She yanked her cart in the opposite direction of the deli and her ex-boyfriend and hurried off down the nearest aisle with Frank struggling to keep up.

Chapter 7

Alexander

Alexander heard the busted muffler on his father's Corolla as the gravel crunched under the tires outside. Given his poor eyesight, he wished his father would stop driving, but at least he always made it home before dark. Not that the town wasn't on the watch for the older man's white Toyota with over two hundred and forty thousand miles on it. If his dad's vision didn't give out soon, he was sure the car would. Not to mention there was not a lot of distance between his trailer and the grocery store or any other store. However, he'd read somewhere that most accidents happen within five miles of home.

Standing the iron upright on the board, Alexander headed outside to find his dad hoisting something off the passenger seat.

"Dad, hang on, let me help you." He speed walked over and discovered what looked like a lumpy bowling ball.

"The ham this year is bigger than most." William stared at it and sighed.

"Why did you do that?" Alexander stood next to his father in the doorway of the car.

"It's what Lucas ordered. We can feed more mouths with it. I believe it'll work out just fine."

Alexander tilted his head. "Dad, you take one side. I'll get the other. How did you even get this in the car?"

"They loaded up for me."

"We'll have to carry this ham like an injured body."

They shuffle-sidestepped around the passenger door and toward the trailer, up the three porch steps, and for once, Alexander was grateful that his dad didn't lock his front door. A quick jiggle of the knob and a shoulder shove allowed the door to swing open.

"I think I can get the refrigerator door open, and we can put it directly inside. However, don't try and remove it when it's time to cook it without letting me help you." Alexander sidestepped toward the refrigerator.

"I'll find someone to help me. You'll still be recovering from surgery. I know. I can ask April."

"I take it you saw her?" He used his pinky and ring finger to grip the refrigerator door handle and swung it open.

They gave the ham a little swing and heaved it onto the nearest shelf, providing a collective sigh.

"Yes." William headed back to the front door. "I think she'll be the perfect addition to the library."

"Addition? Dad, you realize we both can't work there. I'm only going to be out for a few days." He jogged down the steps to catch up with his father. "Not a month, or even weeks."

"Yes." William removed two small grocery bags from the floor on the passenger side of the Corolla and shut the door with his backside. "You should get to decorating for Christmas. With the surgery, you'll be behind." He eyed his son's trailer.

From the first of December to the twenty-sixth, a string of white lights framed his front door with a solid evergreen wreath hung in the middle. And inside, he put up his four foot tree with white lights. "I suppose I could break tradition to keep from veering off schedule. I will do it as soon as I finish my ironing and get the list ready for April tomorrow."

His dad jingled the car keys in his pocket. "You're leaving her a list?"

"More of a rule guide."

"She'll love that." William shook his head and turned toward the trailer.

"What does that mean? Who doesn't appreciate a little guidance?"

His father's only response was a continued shake of his head as he walked up the trailer's porch steps.

"Can I get you anything before I head back home?" Alexander paused as he passed his father's Toyota.

"No, thank you. I'm good for the evening. I believe it's the perfect night for a Christmas movie."

"I'll leave you to it then. Good night, Dad." He took a step toward his trailer.

"Son," his dad called. "I have faith that April can manage the library."

"Yes, Dad." He shook his head before heading to his front door.

Thankfully, Alexander had been able to close the library early. With it regularly closed on Fridays, April wouldn't have to set foot inside until Saturday, and even that would be a short workday. He was happy he could get everything together before his surgery and not have to juggle work on top of it. However, he had one particular task he'd need to complete tonight, no exceptions.

After the sun had set on the day, Alexander finally finished ironing his slacks and button-downs and hung them promptly in their allocated spots in the closet. Then, per tradition, although a day early, Alexander went to his entertainment center—a mid-century credenza and antique-store find—snapped open the right-hand door, and removed his DVD of *A Christmas Story*. He stared at it for a few seconds, emotions flooding with memories of watching it with his mother as a child. It had been her favorite holiday movie, and when he watched it, he could still hear her laughter during specific parts.

Once he placed the movie in the player, he went to his book room off the living room, removed the standing container in the closet, and pulled a red-and-green plastic bin from the low shelf marked Christmas Décor by a strip from his label maker.

Alexander spent a lot of time in the book room. Matching bookcases lined the walls holding classic first-edition books and used books alike. It was rare for him to have a brand-new book because he mostly ordered them for the library and would read them before shelving them in the stacks for public consumption.

In the middle of the small room was an Eames lounge chair and ottoman, the most expensive item in his entire trailer. It was the perfect spot to sit with a cup of tea or coffee and read.

He exited the room with the bin and made his way back to the living room. The Christmas tree went up in the corner between the window and the wall every year. For the rest of the year, the spot remained empty. Even though Alexander was one for traditions and following a schedule, it took a few days to get used to it being bare after the tree was put back away until next Christmas.

With *A Christmas Story* playing in the background, he put the tree together and plugged in the pre-strung lights. "Good, they all work." Next, he removed the classic ball ornaments—gold and silver only—and hung them on the tree, standing back after each one was placed to make sure they were appropriately spaced. For the finishing touches, Alexander added the birch angel tree topper and the golden tree skirt around the base to cover up the plastic stand.

He returned to the Christmas bin and peered inside, spotting his cherry-red (with a hand-stitched manger scene) stocking from his childhood. The last time it'd been hung was when he'd still lived at home with his parents. He didn't see the point in putting it up at his age; yet, something about today caused a bit of Christmas joy to stir inside him. However, he had no idea why. The only thing different about the day was seeing April and helping his father carry in a too-big ham.

Alexander unfolded the red felt stocking. It had been stitched for him by his late mother, and he still found it a beautiful piece of art. He examined the stocking as though for the first time. It had a Christmas tree with a star in the background and woodland creatures crowded around a manger appeared to pop off the fabric. Looking at his credenza, he realized he didn't have a stocking hanger, so he took the loop and hung the stocking from the credenza's doorknob.

Taking a seat on the couch, he crossed his arms, looked at his decorating, and smiled. Then he remembered he still needed to hang the lights around the outside of his front door.

The lights and extension cord were neatly wrapped and secured at the bottom of the plastic box. Scooping them up into his right hand, he approached the front door and pulled it open.

"Judge Dunn." He leaned back, preventing her fist from knocking on his forehead.

"Alexander, how are you? I didn't mean to startle you." The judge wore jeans and a long-sleeved black shirt. Her chili-colored curls framed her face and then some. "I was hopin' you had a moment."

"Sure, as long as you don't mind me hanging up the lights while we talk." He raised the small bundle in his hand.

"Of course not." The judge made herself at home, sitting on the edge of the closest patio chair. "I heard from Lucas and a few others that your dad is doing the ham again this year."

"Yes, it's a tradition."

"It is, but a few of us have some concerns."

"Who is 'a few of us'?" Alexander dragged the vacant patio chair in front of the judge and used it to stand on as he strung the lights over the top of the door frame. "And what type of concerns? It's pretty hard to mess up a ham."

"With your dad's vision, we hoped maybe you could make sure to oversee the ham this year. See, Charlie said he saw him pickin' out spices at the grocery store, and he couldn't read the labels. And when he checked out, he commented on the pepper in his cart, but it was actually poppy seeds."

"That's not too bad."

"He also commented on the cumin, but it was cinnamon."

"That's not good." He winced and stepped off the chair, holding the light string. "Why didn't anyone tell him about his mistakes before he left the store?"

"No one wants to embarrass him and make him feel bad." The judge took a hand and rubbed it across her jeans. "We know he can cook, and we don't want to take away the joy it brings him. Anyone in town is willin' to assist him, but it most likely needs to be someone less noticeable. It would be obvious if people offered to help out of the blue when no one has before."

Alexander clipped the light on the right side of the door and allowed it to dangle. "A valid point. I can help oversee the baking of the ham."

"We know you're having surgery, so we thought maybe April could help your father. You won't be up and about much before the library's celebration."

"I understand that was not a question. However, yes, I'll be right as rain long before then. And I don't need to have April helping my father."

"Keep her in mind. No reason to rush it." Elizabeth stood. "Good luck tomorrow. I hope it goes smoothly." She hurried down the steps without a hug. Normally she hugged everyone, but Alexander was not one to welcome hugs simply because someone was coming or going.

Instead, he gave a wave, and the judge did the same before hurrying back down the driveway to the main road. Elizabeth's house was less than half a mile north, behind the city center, and with such delightful weather it was perfect for a stroll.

He turned back to his front door and pondered about what the judge had said. First, he was grateful that he lived so close to his dad. As he aged, he could easily keep an eye on him. Second, he plugged in the lights and thought they looked the same as every year, good, although early by a day. Third, he tried to push past the bubble of fear forming in his stomach for tomorrow. He couldn't help but wish he had someone to find comfort in during this time, even if just to know they were nearby to hold his hand.

Chapter 8

April

April removed the envelope taped to the library door with her name in cursive on it and slid the key into the lock. The door opened with sticky hesitation, as though it knew it wasn't Alexander.

Allowing Frank's leash to fall onto the carpet, she stepped over the threshold as though entering forbidden territory. The rich mahogany desk nearby held a banker's lamp. A card catalog cabinet made from walnut sat off to the side of the desk. And while she'd been gone for a few years, April was certain it was still functional and in use, even though she hadn't seen Alexander use it yesterday. The children's corner remained decorated in primary colors, bright, though outdated. The reading chairs near the back windows had been reupholstered with a velvety plum fabric. She glanced completely around, noting the chairs were the only welcoming place to sit.

A library was the cheapest form of travel and never excluded a single individual. Or so she thought. For

April's library science thesis, she wrote about worldwide illiteracy. The paper discussed how access to books, or the lack thereof, affected education and opportunities. Her thesis also dove deeply into the benefits of early reading programs for hesitant young readers.

Without Alexander there, Frank was allowed to explore the area, sniffing as he wandered about between the bookcases, his leash dragging behind him.

Ignoring the bank of light switches on the wall near the door because the sunlight filtering in was more than enough, she stepped farther into the library, reaching the middle where the chairs were. Her arms tensed by her side, and her feet stopped in place. The library didn't feel inviting, but she didn't know why. Everything was spotless and in its place. Yet, something caused her to want to grab a book and head elsewhere. How could a library with such historical elements and a few pops of colors feel drab and cold enough to cause April to shiver?

"This place needs a face-lift." April glanced at the clock ticking away on the wall, making her way to the desk.

Removing her gloves, she set them, her purse, and Frank's tote next to the banker's lamp. Then April took the envelope she'd pulled off the door and opened it up. Alexander must've stopped by on his way to surgery and left it for her.

She unfolded the white paper and read the handwritten instructions in near-perfect cursive. The notes all seemed simple enough, maybe even common knowledge, but from what she knew, Alexander had never been away from the library before. She'd heard he didn't take vacation days and treated the library as though it were his only child and no babysitter would ever be good enough.

"I wonder when the last time he left Woolsey was," she murmured to Frank, who had returned to her side. "Oh yes, your bed."

April reached inside her oversize tote and removed a thick fleece blanket. Frank snorted as she laid the makeshift bed at the side of the desk. He approached it, did a circle, then flopped down.

With a smile at Frank's satisfaction with his bed, she returned her attention to the instructions. If she followed Alexander's directions, she'd be rather bored; even reading them caused her to let out a single yawn. Besides, it was December 1, but by looking around, one couldn't tell. She remembered from her visits in the past there had been Christmas decorations, so they must be someplace.

A door with a window stood directly behind the desk, and April went to it, pushed the lever handle down, and swung it open. She flipped the switch on the wall, snapping on the overhead fluorescent light, which caused her to squint until her eyes adjusted.

"Wow, everything is so . . . organized." She blinked.

A metal tanker desk with a 1990s computer monitor was wedged in the corner and it had several stacks of papers, but they were clipped together and placed neatly in three distinct piles. High up on the wall to the left of the desk, a bulletin board held a cluster of cards. Some appeared to be older than others. Holiday cards and birthday cards, their designs different from what she's seen in the stores over the last ten years.

April moved to the open shelves that held labeled boxes. One of them was marked Christmas. *Only one?* She did a double take before removing it with ease from its spot and carried it to the main desk outside of the office. Inside, she located neatly wrapped white lights, a three-foot-tall tree component, and matching silver ornaments.

"I remember more decorations than just *this*."

Frank lifted his head in her direction as she paused at the desk and set her hands on her hips.

Convinced she'd overlooked it, April hurried back into the office and did another search of the shelves for more boxes of Christmas decor. After not finding anything, she sighed. "What a grinch."

"He definitely is," a familiar voice came from outside the office door.

"Aurora?" April asked as she approached the side of the desk.

"I can't believe Alexander finally gave in." Aurora readjusted her cross-body purse.

"So am I, but hopefully, I can bring a little life into this space. Was it always this drab?" April asked. "I don't remember it being like this."

"I'm afraid so."

Aurora kneeled and allowed the bulldog to smell her outstretched hand. "Hey, Frank."

April crossed her arms. "We didn't get a chance to catch up at the grocery store, and I must say, you're looking well these days."

Aurora scratched under Frank's chin and then stood back up. "The girls and I can't complain. They love having Gavin around. We all do."

"Well, I've only been back home a few days, and surprisingly, I've not heard much about the current happenings in the Easton household." April crossed her arms.

"It's been amazing."

"I don't recall—"

Aurora waved her hand. "Oh, Gavin's not a local. He's from Louisiana. He's longtime friends with the judge. We're engaged." She wiggled her ring finger at April.

April stepped forward and examined the diamond-covered band. "Congratulations, I believe my parents mentioned it. When is the wedding?"

"We're not sure yet, we think probably this summer. Trying to decide if we'll have it here or in Jesser Parish. We have a vacation home there."

"He's sort of like the town's unicorn. I think I've only met him once, at the Fourth of July party before Mama Dunn passed away." April took a sip of her coffee from the travel mug on the desk.

"Well, he'll be here for this year's Library's Christmas Celebration."

April eyed the depressing solo box on the desk. "I'm in charge this year, and I believe it will be better than ever before."

"Does Alexander know, or did he agree to this under sedation?" Aurora laughed.

April's face formed a knowing smile. "I'm ironing out the details."

"I know the girls are excited. Gavin missed it last year as he was wrapping stuff up back in Louisiana."

"Hopefully this year it will be one to remember." April sighed. "If I can *spruce* it up a little."

"Your jokes remind me of Alexander." Aurora raised an eyebrow and her smile pulled up on the same side.

"Yikes."

The women shared a laugh as Aurora pulled her cell phone from her back pocket. "Gavin's in Cactus City working a job, and Trinity has the girls today so I can run some errands. I hate to chat and run, but time's ticking away. Can you see if our holds are ready?"

April nodded. "Absolutely. If you let me know where that would be?"

"Same spot as always." Aurora pointed.

April turned around to find a two-shelf bookcase next to the card catalog cabinet labeled Holds. She located the stack of picture books rubber banded with two novels and a slip of paper marked Easton.

All the libraries she had become familiar with in the last handful of years always had a hold shelf where patrons retrieved their books on their own, and for once, she agreed with Alexander's setup. It allowed for more interaction between the reader and the librarian.

April tilted her head. "I can't believe Alexander still checks them out by hand." She picked up the band dater on the desk and examined the paperback thriller on top. "Oh, this one was great."

"You've read it?" Aurora set her purse on the edge of the desk.

"There was a huge independent bookstore across the street from the university. I spent so much time there I should've changed my address to theirs." April removed the check-out card from the inside pocket and punched the return date onto the next line. "Anyways, they had a new release section where they displayed all the newest reads. It made it easier for me to see what was new, instead of having to bring a list or locate them amongst the shelves."

"I wish Alexander would do that." Aurora frowned.

"Have you asked him about incorporating that?"

"I've never bothered. Alexander always has a reason, even if no one else agrees with it."

April removed the next book's card. "Can I ask you what you *don't* like about the library?"

Aurora turned and examined the room, her face contorted at the question. "Honestly?"

"Yes, I promise I won't say a word to Alexander."

"It's not comforting and welcoming. It's sterile, like a hospital waiting room when it should be warm, inviting, and friendly." Aurora crossed her arms and pressed her lips together. "I mean, there're only two chairs to sit in that are comfortable." She pointed at the plum pair. "And the children's section looks straight out of *Romper Room and Friends*. You know, a book club would be great. I've always wanted to be in one."

"I'm in an online book group, and it's so much fun! We live worldwide and do a video meetup once a month. But an in-person book club would be great also." April continued to check out Aurora's books. "Do you want to join my online book club? We always have room for one more."

"Thank you for the invite, but I spend enough time staring at a laptop screen. Maybe you can persuade Alexander to set one up. Both Trinity and Sydney from the post office would be guaranteed club members."

"I'll see what I can do." April handed Aurora the stack of checked-out books. "It'll be one of the many things I'll try and do to liven up this library."

Chapter 9

Alexander

Alexander shifted on the couch, repositioning himself as best he could. His stomach ached for food, and his mind ached for knowledge. He'd already watched every movie he owned since coming home and taking it easy was a challenge for him. Although not heavy, holding a book caused him to sit at a displeasing angle, causing more strain on his healing back.

The longer he sat, the more he noticed how stark his home was. Even with the holiday decor up, it appeared bare and lifeless.

"I've watched too many holiday movies. They over decorate for the sake of charm," he stated to Cora sprawled out on the carpet, soaking up the sun's light that came through the living room window.

He eased himself off the couch and made his way to the window, looking out onto his backyard, or lack thereof. The library was not too far of a walk, maybe half a mile from door to door.

Alexander raised his arm so he could see his watch. The library would only be open for another hour. But he wondered if it was worth pushing himself today. He planned to call April right before closing and let her know that he'd be returning tomorrow regardless of how he felt.

A knock at the front door caused him to jerk, and his hand went to his back to calm the pain his sudden movement created. He made his way to the front door and took a deep breath before opening it. Standing in front of him was a person holding a basket so large it hid their face.

"Hey-llo, Alexander." A head of bleached-blonde hair that belonged to the postal worker popped around the side.

"Sydney, what brings you by?"

"Is the gigantic gift basket not a clue?" She didn't wait for him to move aside and brushed past him, making her way through the entry and into the kitchen. "This thing is heavy." Sydney let it slip from her hands and land on the tiny table with a thump.

"Thank you." He took a quick peek at the basket brimming with items. It was an assortment of Christmas-themed chocolates and chocolate-covered popcorn. "It looks calorie filled."

"What every person needs after surgery." Sydney glanced at the basket.

"A sugar coma?"

She huffed a laugh and turned. "It's not from me. I'll be right back, I brought you a casserole and your mail." Sydney hurried out the front door and toward her Jeep.

Alexander spotted a card tucked into the basket, and without the aid of his letter opener, he ripped open the envelope. He caught himself and noted he indeed was not feeling like himself doing such a messy thing.

He slid the card from the envelope to see it was from Charlie Tow, wishing him well on his recovery. The odd thing was how much Charlie and he had grown in their friendship over the last several years. Not strange that they had a growing friendship, but that it had sprouted in the first place. They were not similar in any way, including their age. However, while not currently in love and had no plans to be, Alexander understood the importance of what was happening in Charlie's life and had stepped up to help him with his recent quest.

"Here you go," Sydney stated, stepping up behind him with two small containers. "I'll put them in the refrigerator for you."

"Wait"—he swiped the mail off the top of the lid—"I'm famished. Could you please leave it out?"

"Sure thing." She turned and set it on the counter near the stove. "It's my cheesy noodle tuna casserole divided it into two smaller dishes so you didn't have to lift a heavy dish."

"You didn't have to go out of your way." Sadness raced through Alexander at the warmth the town was showing him. He was known as the Grinch of Woolsey, yet they were all taking the time during the busy holiday season to make his life more manageable during his recovery.

"It's not out of my way if there's love behind it, not to mention the joy of the Christmas season." Sydney faced him. "You know, every summer when I head up north, I miss this town so very much. And coming back is a nice reminder that there is no other place in the world with such community and love for one's neighbors than here. Us Woolsians are a lucky bunch." She reached her bracelet-covered wrist in his direction and squeezed his left arm. "I know you hate hugs, but you have an excuse right now."

Alexander felt his body start to fold as though he *wanted* a hug.

"Now, do you need anything else before I go? Trash taken out?"

"No, I'm fine. But thank you, Sydney."

"Alrighty then, back to work I go." She hurried past him towards the front door. "Microwave it for about five minutes on medium." Sydney stepped out onto the porch. "I love your fun-size Christmas tree, but don't be afraid to add a little extra. Christmas doesn't bite, I promise."

He wrapped his hand around the door frame, watched Sydney climb into her CJ-7, and heard the engine start.

"Fun-size?" Alexander mumbled as he closed the front door.

As the sound of the Jeep disappeared, he realized that she hadn't mentioned anything about the library, which could only mean one thing, that all was going well, and that was reason to smile.

With his stomach moaning, he popped the lid off the container and placed it in the microwave. At the end of five minutes, his trailer filled with the scent of cheese and warm, fragrant white sauce.

Steam rose from the dish as he used an oven mitt to remove it, grabbed a fork, and carried it to the kitchen table. Yet, before he sat down, he changed his mind. Maybe eating in front of the television wouldn't be the most improper thing in the world. After all, he was recovering and needed a comfy place to sit.

As he took a seat on the couch, his cell phone rang, and he picked it up off the coffee table. The caller ID let Alexander know it was the judge calling.

"Hello, Elizabeth." He eased back on the couch's pillows.

"Hi, Alexander. I didn't mean to disturb you, but as you know, the cacti lightin' is tonight."

"I'm aware." He poked his fork into the dish.

"A few residents have brought it to my attention that we should hold off a few days so that you can attend."

"There is no need to disrupt the schedule for me. Please keep it as is. However, thank you for thinking of me."

"Are you sure?"

"Yes, thank you. I've seen it every year, as far back as I can remember. I believe I can miss it this one time. Have a nice evening. Goodbye."

When he punched end on the phone, doubt crept over him. A tingle of sadness that he would miss the Woolsey tradition surprised him as he took a bite of food. All he could do was hope it passed quickly.

Chapter 10

April

The evening air triggered April to shiver as she zipped up her evergreen-colored jacket and pulled her thin gloves from the pockets. A large crowd of residents had gathered around the circle of saguaros in the city center's parking lot. The lights were out inside the building, making the exterior as dark as the night sky would allow with the full moon. A folding table had been set up on the nearby sidewalk and held several tall thermoses next to a stack of Christmas-themed paper cups.

April waved hello to a few residents as she made her way to the table, and the sound of bats flying overhead filled the air. The labels noted one thermos held apple cider and the other hot chocolate. Whoever set up the station had also included cinnamon sticks and marshmallows to pair with their drink of choice. She poured half a cup of hot chocolate and spooned in two scoops of mini marshmallows before heading toward the saguaro cacti.

Glancing down the road, April noticed two horses trotting towards the parking lot. On them were Camden and Trinity, with Jolie sitting nestled against the front of her mom. While the city center had parking spots, it also had a hitching post off to the left from who knows how many years ago.

A few more residents strolled in, undoubtedly leaving their cars back at home. The cloudless sky and temperature hovering around sixty were enough for a desert dweller to bundle up. Even if there was no snow or really anything in the Arizona landscape that looked like Christmas, it was the perfect opportunity to feel a part of the holiday season by wrapping oneself up in warm clothing.

Elizabeth appeared around the corner of the building, coming from the direction of her house, carrying a sizable reusable grocery bag. April stepped onto the sidewalk as the judge set the bag at the end of the table.

"Hi, Elizabeth." April sipped her hot chocolate, the marshmallows tapping against the top of her lip.

Elizabeth beamed a grin in her direction. "April, correct?"

She nodded and took another drink of hot chocolate, making sure there were no leftover marshmallow bits stuck to her lip.

"We're all grateful you're takin' over the library duties for Alexander." The judge removed two large Christmas tree-shaped plates displaying snowmen, reindeer, and sleigh-shaped decorated cookies. "Please, help yourself." She pointed.

April tilted her head and eyed them. "They look scrumptious." She selected a snowman and bit off its hat.

"I saw you run out of here in a hurry after work today"—the judge grabbed a sleigh cookie and crossed her arm supporting her hand—"with your dog, but you didn't bring him tonight?"

"I figured he could use some alone time." She laughed. "He's back at my parents' house."

"So what had you in such a hurry?"

April leaned in as though Alexander might be able to hear her. "I'm working up some plans to make the library . . . more festive. Although, I'm not sure how Alexander will feel about it all." She broke off another nibble of the snowman. "I'm going for a rip-off-the-Band-Aid approach."

"I suspect that might be the only way." Elizabeth looked out at the crowd continuing to form. "Oh, I see Sydney; I heard she visited with Alexander earlier today. Please excuse me." She hurried off with half a sleigh cookie in her hand.

April continued to make the snowman disappear as she wondered if Alexander could see anything from his place of the cacti lighting. She looked in the direction of his trailer but only could make out the roofline.

"Short Stuff Gardner!"

April paused, the remaining bottom of the snowman on her lips. *No!* She pressed her eyes tightly closed before opening them as she turned around. "Lucas, you made it."

He approached the table and snatched up a cookie. Without looking at it, he took a bite. "Why not? Nothing else to do tonight. Unless you want to come over to my place? We could"—he winked—"catch up."

April caught herself before her head shook vigorously in a resounding *no*. Instead, she reached for a frosted white sleigh and shoved nearly half of it into her mouth. Then, holding up a finger, motioning that she couldn't answer right at the moment, she peeked around him and spotted William making his way into the parking lot on foot.

"Sorry, maybe later. I must speak with William," she mumbled through the crumbs and hurried off.

Approaching William, she gave a quick wave to get his attention, but then she remembered William's vision issues. She polished off the cookie before she made it to Alexander's dad.

"How is your son doing?" April asked once they were close enough.

"Ah, Little April, hello. Alexander is doing well, but it's a shame he's going to miss this. I don't think he ever has in his lifetime."

April placed her hand on her heart as though it hurt with sadness for Alexander. "There's no way we can get him here? Can he walk this far?"

"Oh, I believe he could. However, when I stopped by to check on him, he shooed me off. And when I pressed him, he said he was too tired."

"You're still in charge of flipping the switch for the lights." April smiled.

William nodded and adjusted his well-worn veteran's hat.

She'd spotted what might be the best mode of transportation for someone recovering from back surgery that would get Alexander to the city center. "Can you delay the lighting by about ten minutes? I have a plan."

"Yes, of course." William's face warmed with delight.

"Thanks." She patted Mr. Adams on the shoulder and moved past him to find the driver of the vehicle.

Chapter 11

April

April rapped her fist in the middle of Alexander's generically plain wreath on the door and stepped back. While she noticed the Christmas lights that framed the front door, she could only assume through the window's closed, but sheer curtains, that the glistening of lights inside was on a small tree.

The door eased open, and Alexander, dressed in sweat bottoms and a black T-shirt, appeared.

"Hi, sorry to disturb you," she stuttered, shaken by him looking so cute. "I didn't want you to miss the cacti lighting."

"I'm fine," he paused and rested his hand on the doorknob. "Even if I wanted to go, getting into the car is painful, and walking would take too long."

"That's what I was thinking, so I figured it out." April stepped aside and pointed out into his driveway.

"Is that the Miller's golf cart?" He squinted out into the darkness of the driveway.

She smiled and rubbed her gloved hands together, trying her best to ignore the fact that seeing Alexander dressed, well, un-Alexander made her even more attracted to him. Not that she wasn't before, yet he'd always seemed out of her reach until right at that moment.

"April?"

"What did you say?" She blinked firmly, trying to rid the thoughts of what could but never would happen from her brain. "It's super easy to get in and out of, and I have your dad waiting to flip the switch."

He glanced around her and then looked down at himself. "I'm not dressed for it."

"No one cares, you're recovering. Plus, it's dark out." She bit her lower lip. "Come on. You can't miss out on the festivities. The judge even brought her sugar cookies."

His eyes widened, and a smile attempted to twitch across his lips. "Those cookies are delicious."

"And they're doctor recommended for back surgery healing." April looked past him and into his living room, spotting the TV with a black-and-white Christmas movie playing on it.

"Now you're making up stuff." He crossed his arms. "Fine. Suppose you'd be kind enough as to give me a minute, or three, to put on my jacket and shoes. It's not an easy task."

"Let me help you. I understand what you're going through. My mom had a similar surgery when I was a teenager." She started to step forward. "However, I'll need to come inside to help."

"Right." He moved behind the door. "Honestly, I can manage."

Waving him off, she entered. Being close to him allowed her to smell the scent of vanilla and cedarwood. When April looked around, she couldn't help but notice the trailer was as bare as a horse's bottom. It would be lifeless if it wasn't for the Christmas tree and cat curled up on the couch, though April was impressed by the style of furniture in his home. It was like walking into the television while *Mad Men* was on.

"What's your cat's name?" April spun around but left her hand pointing at the couch. "Is it Garfield? Because it looks just like him."

Alexander chuckled. "It's Cora." Then he paused and turned his head. "I guess I never noticed the resemblance."

April went to the cat, whose head rose at the new visitor, and gave it a quick pet. "Where are your coat and shoes?"

"Cora doesn't wear any."

She found herself blushing to keep from feeling silly. "Good one."

"I can get them. Please give me a minute."

April watched him make his way down the hall, returning with a dark tan jacket and a pair of gray tennis shoes. She tried not to let her face show the shock of seeing Alexander holding those types of shoes.

"Here, let's keep you standing, and I'll put them on for you." She took the shoes from him and kneeled at his feet. "Less bending is probably best. Use my shoulder to stabilize yourself."

Alexander lifted his right foot simultaneously as he gently set his hand on her shoulder. April felt her body jitter at his touch and tried to ignore it. She didn't have feelings for Alexander Adams. It just wasn't possible.

"Other foot," she instructed after moving to his left foot.

"Are you double knotting my laces?" he asked.

"Yes, sorry, a habit from my babysitting days." She stood up and assisted him with his coat. "Don't worry. I'll come back with you and help you remove these."

"Thank you, I appreciate it. However, please don't go out of your way." Alexander followed behind her. "Let me get my keys."

She stopped and turned around just as Alexander reached for them off the hook on the wall next to the front door. With his face close to hers, she froze, scared yet delighted. She was not frightened by him but worried about being that close to him and to his lips. She wanted to close her eyes, bury her face in his scent. And if April didn't move, she might do exactly that.

"Excuse my reach," he said, soft and low.

"It's alright," she whispered and looked down.

Once the door was locked, they made their way to the golf cart. April walked close enough for their shoulders to tap, just in case he might need her help. She stood by as he slid into the passenger side of the cart.

"You know how to drive one of these?" he asked as she sat on the driver's side.

"I got it here." She shrugged and turned the key into the on position. "I'll drive nice."

She eased her foot onto the gas pedal, slowly making their way onto the pavement leading to the city center.

April parked the golf cart in the fire lane near the table set up with the goodies. The residents noticed Alexander and gave him friendly waves and welcomes.

William stood at the edge of the circle containing the cacti, holding the two extension cords as though he were Clark Griswold. "Thank you all for coming, and I'm glad my son could make it. Here in Woolsey, we have many things to be grateful for this year. And like every year, it's because of our strong community values and caring neighbors. May this cacti lighting bring the joy of the holiday season to you and your family, friends, and loved ones. On the count of three, let us share a Merry Christmas."

April stood next to Alexander, and the rest of the residents gathered around and focused on the five saguaros.

"One, two," the town called out, "three. Merry Christmas!"

The cacti, with at least two arms, each shone brightly with green, blue, red, orange, and yellow lights. Everyone clapped, and some pointed with delight. It was a sight to behold, even after many years of the same thing. The glow cast shadows of Christmas colors on the faces of people closest to it. When April turned to smile at Alexander, she caught him staring with a frozen smile on his face.

"It's pretty," she said to him.

All he did was nod, like a shocked child spotting Santa on Christmas Eve. April watched him, soaking up the joy his face projected. The urge to reach down and hold his hand was a thought she never expected.

"Can I get you a cookie and something to drink?" she offered and stepped away from him as though he were the North Pole and the magnetic force was too strong.

He turned to her, the smile still plastered to his lips. "No, but thank you for making me come. It really wouldn't feel like Christmas if I'd missed it."

"You're welcome." She blushed, grateful for the dark of night that hid it.

"Did you see the mountain cactus?" Alexander pointed up and out into the distance.

April did her best to follow his finger, leaning closer toward him. "Oh, yeah."

On the top of the shortest mountain in Woolsey, there grew a cactus that mysteriously was decorated with Christmas lights every December.

"I didn't know if the tradition continued after I left for college. My parents never mentioned it." April tilted her head as though it would help her see better.

"Tradition is tradition. I do worry about what the future holds for it." Alexander's hand moved inside of his pocket.

"You don't think the younger residents will take over the Christmas mystery?"

"As long as I have kids, the tradition will continue," Alexander said without looking at her.

April's vision went to the ground. The statement was unexpected and only made her want to ask a million more questions. She'd always assumed she knew everything there was to know about Alexander—until now. And that meant big trouble for her heart.

Chapter 12

Alexander

Alexander stepped inside the city center the next morning as Keith held the door open.

"Surprised to see you out and about," Keith stated, letting go of the door and moving his hand to rest on his belt.

Alexander was still, after several years, not used to seeing Keith as the city center's guard. The town knew full well the building didn't need security. But they didn't want to lose any more long-term residents, and Keith provided support in more ways than only as a guard. His skill set included handling building repairs, anything from a broken air conditioner to plumbing issues in the bathroom.

"I'm only stopping by for a quick check-in."

"So you heard," Keith stated.

Alexander's vision darted to the open library door. "Heard about?"

"April's great plans for the Christmas celebration. She's been decorating up a storm, not to mention she has some ideas perfect for the future of the library." Keith glanced over his shoulder.

How much trouble could she have caused in two days?

Alexander rigidly hurried toward the library door and received his answer as soon as he stepped over the threshold.

His jaw hinged open, and his eyes widened at the sight. "Are there any holiday decorations left at the store, or are they all here?"

April popped her head up over a nearby book-case, a stack of books in her hands. She laughed and then smiled. "What are you talking about?" As she approached, she spun back around and looked in the direction he was staring in.

"Christmas exploded in here!" his voice screeched, and he brought his hand to his mouth, unaware it could make such a horrid sound.

In the center of the library was not any regular Christmas tree but a white plastic one with blue-and-gold decorations. Taped to the walls were giant cutout paper reindeer and Santas. How confusing it must be for a child to see multiple Santas in the same place. Flashing red and green Christmas presents sat on his desk, and near the window, a whirring noise came from an eight-foot-tall inflatable dinosaur with a Santa hat on that barely cleared the ceiling.

"You don't like it?" She lowered the stack of books in her hand, appearing to nearly drop them. "I worked so hard."

"I can see you worked hard, yet it's . . ." Alexander shoved his hands so deep into his pockets he could feel lint stuck to the stitching in the corner. "I'm going to be honest. It's tacky. For starters, a dinosaur is not Christmas, nor does it belong inside, let alone with a Santa hat on. This is not the Arizona Museum of Natural History."

April's forehead wrinkled, and she allowed the books to fall from her hands onto a nearby study table. He winced at the sound of the books' possible damage.

She frowned and hurried past him to the bulldog sitting on a blanket by his desk. Alexander pointed yet again. "What's he doing here?"

"You said Frank can be here."

"And why does he always look like a disgruntled employee?"

"That's uncalled for. He's a bulldog. They come disgruntle." April's knee-length floral-print dress looked as though it had tulle under it, puffing it wide, causing her to appear like a princess. "Should you be here? I mean, you're supposed to be home healing."

All she needed was a tiara, which he assumed she had. He couldn't believe April had returned to dusty, plain ole Woolsey since it was seemingly an unfit match—but then again, so was he. It took a great deal of work to keep the dirt of the desert from causing problems with his attire, in his home, and the library. However, her beauty had distracted him enough in high school that he was not surprised to find it still did the same today.

"Did your doctor even clear you?" April glanced up at him from petting the bulldog.

"I don't need a note to come into *my* library. Let us not forget I went to the cacti lighting last night. Remember, you kidnapped me in the golf cart?"

"Let's not be overdramatic, Alexander." April stood and pressed her hands onto her dress to ensure it stayed in place. "Last night, you only walked a few steps. You didn't run a marathon. And I most certainly didn't kidnap you."

"I feel as though you've kidnapped the library." Alexander motioned his hand, palm up around the room. "It looks like the set rejections of a Christmas movie gone wrong."

"Are you always this rude, or is it your pain medication?"

Alexander crossed his arms. "This is *my* library."

April stomped over to him and drew close enough for him to see the sparkle in her pearl pink lip gloss. "No, the library belongs to the town. And residents have been talking."

"Talking?" A sharp pain in his back caused him to wince.

"Yes, they want something inviting, something different." She crossed her arms, and her posture stiffened, making her appear as though she was taller than him.

"Well." He pinched his eyes closed as the pain radiated. Before his mind could process the feeling, he opened his eyes to find April's hand, her nails a Christmas red

80

with tiny white snowflakes on them, resting against the base of her neck.

"Sorry, I tried to help." Her hand fell to her side as she took a step backward.

Alexander pushed through the fog of pain. "This is the opposite of inviting. Christmas should be classic, simple. Instead, this is going to give someone a migraine."

Alexander had to move his vision from April. She looked like she was about to cry. However, it was as though his eyes were glued in place. Instead, he did the only thing his body would allow. He turned and walked toward the door of the library. "I want this gone by tomorrow—including the dog. I've decided he can't stay. I'll be back working full time, and I don't want to clean up after you."

He heard April stomping up behind him. "After *me*? I'm doing *you* a favor. And Frank is a service dog, so he stays."

"I don't understand why you need a service dog now that you're back here." Alexander held his ground, crossing his arms. "It's not the city."

"Alexander, is everything alright?" Keith asked as he hurried past him.

"Everything is swell." His back ached, and all he wanted to do was lie on his side to alleviate the pain. Yet, as he made it out of the center, out of the parking lot, and past the lighted cacti, something else hurt—his heart. Alexander thought of last night when he and April had stood next to each other, enjoying the glow of holiday lights. And even though he couldn't make out any illumination in the daytime, he glanced in the distance at the cactus on top of the mountain.

The sun warmed his cheeks as he made his way home. The walk seemed longer than usual, and he wanted a nap by the time he reached his front door. However, the sound of his father calling out across the yard let him know it was doubtful.

"Alexander!" William shouted. "Alexander!"

"Not now, Dad. I want to rest." Alexander shoved the key into the door's lock.

If his father wanted to talk to him, he could at least be sitting down. At this juncture, his old man had more energy and flexibility.

Leaving the front door open, Alexander lowered himself onto the couch and took the front of his wing-tip shoe to the heel of the other and removed them without having to bend down. With his feet up on the couch, his father walked through the front door.

"Why did you do that to Little April?" William accused.

"How do *you* already know?" *I don't walk that slowly.* Alexander rested his head on the couch pillow. "I didn't do anything. It's my library, and she made it look like a Christmas yard sale. There is a *dinosaur* with a Santa hat on."

"She's trying to bring joy to the library. Something fresh. Something that's been missing for far too many years."

His dad leaned over the back of the couch, his arms pressed against his hips.

"What are you talking about? Everyone loves the library."

"Yes, they love the books but nothing else about it."

Alexander sighed and sat up. "I don't understand."

His dad walked around the couch and motioned his son to move his feet so he could sit. Alexander held a grumble in his cheeks as he eased his feet toward him.

"Have you ever felt Christmas?" William grabbed his jeans at the thighs as he lowered onto the couch.

"You're not going to start singing, are you?"

His father huffed. "No. Have you felt the spirit of hope during the holiday season? The way the lights glisten and illuminate, showing off the silhouette of beauty?"

Alexander swallowed, and every inch of it was sharp and jagged going down, like a pine cone.

"Son, if you don't feel the utter joy of Christmas, then I suggest you start. It's been too long."

He looked at his tree in the living room. "I don't know what you could possibly be referring to."

"I miss your mother, too. And I can't fix the fact that she's not here to celebrate, but don't go all humbug because of it. She wouldn't want you to."

Chapter 13

April

April couldn't allow anyone to see the tears streaming over her cheeks, so she remained hidden in the library long after the city center had locked its doors for the night. Once closed and empty, with the exception of her and Frank, April went to work removing every last decoration she'd put up and made three trips to the dumpster out back. The humiliation and embarrassment clouded her judgment, and she didn't think about taking it to a donation site (not that one was nearby) until after it hit the bottom of the dumpster.

She flopped into one of the plum chairs in the center of the room and leaned her head back like she was about to get it washed at a salon's uncomfortable sink.

"What did I do so wrong?" she asked the ceiling and Frank, who she heard stretch and shake his body.

April didn't recall a teenaged Alexander being smug about Christmas. In fact, she distinctly remembered him coming to school with containers full of gingerbread and sugar cookies and cards with candy canes taped to the envelopes.

Of course, the way the cookies were decorated led everyone to understand that Mrs. Adams had spent a great deal of time on them. Sadly, teenagers showed little regard as they shoved them down their throats, green and red sprinkles sticking to the corners of their mouths. And she'd been one of them.

Frank wandered over to April and used her leg as a rubbing post for his itchy muzzle. She reached a hand down and patted him on his head. Continuing to think back to those high school memories, April pulled another from her mind: Alexander's Christmas cards and how vintage they were year after year.

"That's it!" April leaped from the chair. "He's old-fashioned. Old school." She smiled. "I know how to make this right."

After checking the clock on the wall, she snatched her purse, attached Frank's leash to his collar, and hurried out of the library like she was running late for a Christmas flight.

The drive took about an hour and a half to get back into town. Thankfully, the home improvement store employee had tied the tree on properly, and she didn't have to worry about it flying off during the drive. She had zero time for a redo.

Yet, as April drove closer towards the city center's parking lot, she spotted someone exiting the building and climbing into a truck. "Who would be at the center this late? It's closed."

Easing her car parallel to the city center's curb, she watched the vehicle speed away, swearing it was Charlie Tow's truck.

"Why would Charlie be here?" April shut off the car and climbed out but stuck her head back inside. "You stay here, Frank," she said to the bulldog sitting in the passenger seat with his harness clipped to the seat belt contraption.

He glanced out the side window toward the center and then back at her, his one bottom tooth hooked outside of his top lip. April muffled a laugh at Frank's perpetually perturbed face.

She shut the car's door, then stood on her tippy toes to see the roof of her car, and studied first the tree and then the city center's front doors. Then, taking her keys, she went to the main doors, unlocked them, and found a large rock nearby to prop it open.

Back at the car, the twine was tight and didn't leave much wiggle room to undo it. She used her key and rubbed it back and forth until it broke free, sending a spray of needles into the air with it. Bringing her hands to her hips, she sighed. She was too short to pull it off the back or the front, and she couldn't reach the middle of the hood to grab the trunk to remove it sideways from the car.

She opened the driver-side door and climbed onto the frame, widening her stance for balance. But even higher up, she couldn't quite get a good enough grip.

"How do short people ever get trees off their cars?" she wondered aloud. April hopped down and rubbed the back of her neck from the strain. "The bat!"

She opened the back door and felt around the floorboard until she located the baseball bat. Her father had insisted she take it to college with her (to use as a weapon for defense) since Frank was a service dog and not a guard dog, although his snoring could easily scare off just about anyone. Only she'd never remembered to bring the bat inside.

Climbing back onto the car door sill, she took the bat and pushed it to the middle of the tree, nudging the trunk. Giving it a final push, the tree rolled off the car's roof and onto the sidewalk on the other side with a whoosh.

She clenched her jaw, hopped down, and scurried around the bumper. April hoisted it up to standing and examined the tree. "I hope I didn't destroy it."

Leaning back to look, and although there was not much light, the tree looked to have survived the fall.

Giving the tree a giant hug, she heaved it off the ground and entered the city center. Then upon reaching the library door, she leaned the tree against the wall. After removing the key and unlocking the door, she itched the front of her neck where the tree's needles had rubbed against the skin.

With another big hug, she lifted the tree and carried it into the center of the library. She wished the tree lot hadn't run out of netting to wrap it up, but luckily there was no noticeable damage.

April rested the tree against a bookcase, hurried back to the car to retrieve three large bags, and then returned for a final time to bring Frank inside.

Once Frank had made himself at home on his blanket, April removed her scarf and puffy jacket and set to work on getting the tree stand in place. Without another set of hands, she'd have to manage to stabilize the tree by herself, which would be a challenge, as the past had proven.

While in college, April decorated mini versions of everything, and when she was back home in Woolsey, her dad always did the bulk of the work. The white plastic tree she'd initially gone with was anything but heavy. Yet, whatever it took, she had to make this right with Alexander.

Untwisting the bolts in the stand, she made room for the tree's trunk. Grabbing the trunk and trying her best to keep from being stabbed in the eyeball by a branch, she hoisted it into the stand. Unfortunately, April miscalculated the trunk's width, and the bottom of the tree nearly bounced when it hit the top of the bolts.

As silly as it sounded, April wanted to cry, her energy and strength was weaning. Hoisting the tree back up enough to clear the stand, she propped it up against the bookcase, redid the bolts, and tried again. Thankfully, this time, she got it right.

She allowed the tree to rest against her while she held it with one hand and twisted the bolts to secure it in place. After all three were tight, she stood up and stepped back only to find the tree leaned at a thirty-degree angle.

"Crap!" April stomped her right foot.

After three more attempts to straighten the tree, she was satisfied. "Yay! Finally, you're straight." She clapped her hands together. "Now it's time to decorate."

Yawning, April glanced at the clock on the wall, eleven fifteen. No wonder she was tired, not to mention hungry. She had no time to waste, though, even for a quick bite to eat.

Luckily, April had some antique pieces from her parents' ornament collection. They hadn't used them since her first memories of Christmas, and even then, she only saw them in her baby photos. But she knew they were exactly what the tree needed to make it memorable for Alexander.

She unloaded the shopping bags of ornaments she purchased at the store along with the box from her parents' garage. Before heading to Cactus City, she'd popped several bags of popcorn to string, but alas, she hadn't realized that the popcorn was a powdery cheese flavor, so it was a bust. Everything else she put on the tree had a traditional, vintage feel—even if she bought many of them brand-new tonight. She added glass reflector ornaments in green, blue, and red. While April might be getting some of the histories intermingled, it would be as *Christmas Carol* classic as possible.

The groan of her stomach echoed in the emptiness of the library and was so loud that it caused Frank's head to rise from the blanket. There must be something in the center's tiny shared break room. She patted her leg and called the bulldog to follow her.

Swinging open three cupboard doors, April got on her tippy toes to see around the coffee mugs and stacks of paper plates.

"Aha!" The commotion of joy startled Frank, and the dog let out two short barks. "Popcorn."

April removed the three-pack box of microwavable popcorn and smiled when she saw it was buttered and not cheesy—it would have to do. Next to the box of popcorn were two packets of tuna and a box of crackers.

"Frank, I think we found our dinner." She snatched up the snacks and wiggled them at the dog as though he understood. "We'll replace all this tomorrow."

After popping the bags of popcorn, she found a plastic bag and loaded up everything she'd located, then headed back to the library with Frank by her side. April spread several napkins at the kid's table in the library's corner and prepared a snack for both of them.

With two satisfied bellies, April returned to the tree and added the tin candle holders with tiny cream candles and a glistening golden Bethlehem star to complete the look. Then, she sat in one of the plum chairs to begin the tedious task of stringing popcorn. By the time she'd finished, her eyes were tired, her fingers sore and greasy, and the clock on the wall read one in the morning.

After shutting off the lights and locking up, April looked back and marveled at how wonderfully cozy the tree looked, even if it was the only thing that reminded readers it was Christmastime in the library.

On the drive to her parents' house, she remembered she'd have to let Alexander know she'd seen Charlie fleeing into the night. Tomorrow morning, she'd have to finish putting up the rest of the decorations. And right before Alexander arrived, she'd light the candles on the tree, perfecting the classic Christmas scene. She felt a flutter in her chest, thinking about seeing his reaction.

Chapter 14

Alexander

As usual, Alexander woke before his alarm could alert him, noting he'd received enough sleep not to need to set one. While his back was still recovering and he had an upcoming month of physical therapy, he couldn't sit around his house anymore. He missed the library. He missed the books and readers, and most of all, he had to fix the horrendous mess of Christmas decorations April had put up. He'd even left a message on her cell phone just before the library closed yesterday to let her know her help would no longer be needed.

The sunshine was blocked by rolling puffy clouds that stretched for miles in the distance as he approached the parking lot of the city center and spotted April's car. *Hopefully, she's only there to take down the decorations.*

Keith held the door open for Alexander as he came inside. "Good morning, Alexander."

"Morning." Alexander hurried past without any other pleasantries. He didn't have time to chat. He had work to do.

His eyes grew wide with each step closer to the open library door. Gone were the tacky decorations on the walls and the white tree. In its place was a full Douglas fir, brimming with classic ornaments—he blinked—and tiny lit candles.

"Hello, Alexander," April said, appearing from the office to the left.

"Did you not get my message?"

April tilted her head. "No, but I hope you like what I've done. Classic and simple." A smile inched on her lips as she stared at him with the tree behind her.

And then the tree grew brighter over her right shoulder, and he moved past her with rigid steps. "It's on fire!" Alexander shouted.

April's head snapped around. "Oh no, it must be the darn butter popcorn!"

Alexander moved closer to the tree as swiftly as he could, but he had nothing to put out the growing fire. "How could you get a real tree? This is Arizona; the trees are dry as heck."

"I was trying to do a nice thing after you got so upset with me for decorating in the first place." April's hands were outstretched at the tree. "Should we call the Hackenbergs?"

"No time! There's a fire extinguisher near the office door on the wall." Alexander pointed.

April ran to it, ripped it from the wall, and hurried over. She pulled the pin out and aimed it at the tree. With a long burst, white powder shot from the nozzle and covered the tree and everything on it.

"Hey," April said as she lowered the extinguisher, "now you have a flocked tree."

"You're trying to make jokes?" Alexander slowly turned to her, his head tilted.

"I'm trying to put a positive spin on the situation." She put her hand up in a stop motion toward the dog that rose by the side of his desk. "My parents' ornaments were on there."

"You almost set the entire library on fire!"

"It was a small fire from a small candle. The butter popcorn was probably not the best idea, but I was trying. Maybe you should be grateful I went out of my way to do this for you." April pointed at what remained of the tree. It looked fuller with the dripping foam.

"I would assert that the candles were a poor choice," he exhaled and reached for a nearby chair. "I am sorry about the ornaments."

"Thank you. How is your back?" April's hand stretched out as he lowered into the reading chair. "You really should take it easy. I have plenty of time to stay and help."

He couldn't admit he needed help, even if it would be nice. However, April Gardner was not the one to give it to him. Everything she touched ended in disaster. Plus, she had the dog.

"Do I smell tuna?" Alexander directed his nose into the air.

April's eyes wandered as she set the extinguisher on top of the bookcase. Clearly, she was avoiding the question. It must be the dog smelling like tuna.

"I can manage the library on my own. Now, I have plenty to do, so you must excuse me. And please don't bring your dog in here again. I've changed my mind about him." Alexander attempted to stand, but the pain caused him to wince and lean back in the chair.

"Frank comes with me. He's a service dog, regardless of if I'm in the city or not. And you clearly can't be working. You need to take it easy." April clasped her hands together and rested them in front of her blue chiffon dress. "Now, how about we make a plan?"

He eased to the right. "Plan?" The only plan he needed was to heal up, so he didn't need to rely on anyone. And surely one that didn't involve April's beauty distracting him either.

"Yes." April took a seat in the chair nearest him. "I know you're too stubborn to admit you need my help, as does this library." She looked around. "Not to mention the upcoming celebration."

He crossed his arms, but the motion caused the pain to increase, therefore he rested his hands on top of his knees instead. "You do make a valid point. My plate is currently full of things to accomplish."

"And the residents have been talking to me. I'm not sure if they've mentioned it to you, but they want to see some changes here."

He was aware. However, maybe she could provide more information. "Changes?"

"Yes, and I'm the person to help you implement them."

"Why would you assume such a thing?" His forehead creased.

"Because I just finished my degree, meaning my knowledge in library science is current, and I'm well aware of what modern libraries have to offer."

He ran his tongue over his teeth.

"Am I so horrible that you can't stand to spend a few weeks with me?" April lowered her head and ran the charm on her necklace back and forth on the chain. "And Frank?"

Alexander sighed. He hadn't deliberately wanted to make her feel bad, but she was remarkably different from him, and honesty was always the best policy. The last thing he needed in his life was to give any more thought to change, and he most certainly didn't need to spend more time with *her*.

"Here's what we'll do." Alexander held up his finger. "Since I need to take it easy, and I'm not healing as quickly as I'd like, I suppose we can create a plan for the library, to defend its authenticity and carry the celebration out on time."

April folded her hands together in her lap. "This feels very *Home Alone*." She smiled.

"Home-a-who?"

Her head pulled back, allowing her chin to sink into her neck. "*Home Alone*, the famous Christmas movie from the nineties."

"I didn't have access to a lot of extras growing up. And television was not a priority."

"But it's been on television for years . . . and on rental . . . *and* streaming. Surely you've seen it by now."

"Now that you speak of it, I believe I've heard of it, but it's a children's movie?"

"It's a classic." April pressed her lips together. "You read classic novels, right?"

Alexander thought about how this might be a trap, but he answered anyway. "Yes."

"It's the perfect family movie. I know. Let's show it during our Christmas celebration."

When did the library become ours? "The library doesn't have a television. We have books."

She stood up and walked over to the large blank white wall on the other side of the library. "We can show it here, with a projector. I saw one in the office."

"I must reiterate, the library is not for movies."

"Actually, it is. Most libraries offer movies and music to check out."

"Why?"

"Because similar to your childhood and mine, not everyone can afford to have all the latest and greatest."

He slumped over. Alexander had never once thought about the library as a helping hand. More so, he thought of it as a place to access books for education and for those who didn't have much storage in their house to keep them. While he did grow up in a less-than-middle-class family, he always saw the library as a fun place to be where he could walk in empty-handed and come away with a huge stack of books—that wasn't possible for him at a bookstore. How had he failed to notice the library in such a way before?

"I know that libraries, well books in general, have a hard time these days competing against movies and television. Therefore, I'm hoping that with a well-stocked place for people to explore all a library has to offer, that might change," April said. "Bring more people in to search for what they want."

"What do you propose we do?" His heart felt warm as it radiated through him. Could he be feeling excitement?

"Let me get my notepad." With a spring in her step, like a child skipping along with their best friend, she returned and sat next to him in the other plum chair. The scent of lemon and sugar danced from her. "For example, I thought we could set up a section of books made into movies. We could showcase the book and movie together and invite discussions on the outcomes during a reader get-together."

He scratched at the back of his hair. "That idea has possibilities."

"Wonderful." April's expression went from delightful to suspicion as she tapped the pen to her lip. "I also wanted to talk to you about Charlie Tow."

"I figured someone would find out about that."

Chapter 15

April

April couldn't recall the last time she'd gone through so many emotions at once. In the morning, she'd hurried to the library with the joy of surprising Alexander and hopefully mending what friendship they had. Yet, with her focus distracted, she'd created a bigger mess than before. She only wanted to do something good for the town and bring more life to the library.

Even sitting down with Alexander to go over possible upgrades to the library, April was stuck staring at the fire extinguisher-flocked tree. But when the subject switched to Charlie, she'd turned giddy with intrigue when he told her what had happened. And it only caused her to realize how sweet Alexander could be, and she didn't like it one bit because it only made her want to know more about who he really was.

Throughout the rest of the day, Alexander sat uncomfortably in the library chair while she cleaned up the aftermath of the fire and lugged the burnt tree out to the trash with the help of Keith. Then, when Alexander inquired more about the details of Frank's skills as a therapy dog, she explained them at length. She thought he would've judged her as being weak or unable to handle change, but he was understandingly kind. And when she turned out of the parking lot of the city center, the realization of why Alexander had been kind made sense. He hated change, and it was apparent in the library and its lack of modernizing in so many ways. Change created anxiety in him, and he'd been able to completely avoid the mental health issue by keeping the library exactly as he wanted it.

For now, she would focus on the upcoming Christmas celebration and help reshape the library so residents knew they'd been heard. Plus, she needed several things to focus on with regard to Alexander so she didn't notice how he smelled like vanilla and cedarwood. Or how when he smiled, it was slightly crooked. And how he laid out his lunch like a butler with a ruler, precisely positioned. She wondered what it would be like to sit with him in front of a warm fire, sipping a glass of pinot grigio and reading a book.

The day had utterly exhausted her, and the last thing she wanted to do was cook dinner. Turning off SR 287, April headed to Breakfast, Lunch, Dinner & Everything in Between and found the lot packed. Luckily, she was able to park her car in the last available spot.

"I'll be right back, Frank." She gave the dog a rub around the ear and then climbed out of the car. Thankful she could leave him in the car for a few minutes without worrying about the heat. Although it was a brisk forty-three degrees and the sun had set, she still cracked the windows just in case.

As she opened the door of the restaurant, bells jingled and mixed with the chatter of conversations. The scent of gravy and warm bread filled her nose, and she smiled with the delight of the aroma. She spotted Luis standing at a table, conversing with the diners. When he looked over and saw her, he gave a wave. April waved back and readjusted her purse.

"I'm afraid there are no empty tables," Luis said as he approached.

"No worries, I'm getting it to go." April smiled.

"Go over and tell Lil what you want," he glanced over towards the bar counter, "it looks like there is an open seat. Rest your feet for a few minutes."

A bell rang at the kitchen's ledge, and a waitress hurried over and swiped up the two plates. She was grateful for her past employment here but also glad she didn't have to stand on her feet all day anymore.

"April, what can I make you?" Lillian peeked through the serving window.

"What's the soup of the day?" April climbed onto the vacant barstool.

"Creamy potato," Lillian said over the sizzle of the grill.

"Perfect for a cold night. I'll take that to go, please."

"Sure thing." Lillian spun around and disappeared behind the frame.

"I heard about the fire, Short Stuff Gardner."

Lucas.

"So did I," Vince, to her left, added.

"Hi, Vince, Lucas."

Vince worked as a teacher at the high school and was somewhat less annoying than Lucas, or at the most, wasn't an ex-boyfriend.

"No one came into the library all day, yet you know about it," April stated.

"Dolores said she spotted a half-burned Christmas tree being carried out to the dumpster." Vince held his fork above his plate of meatloaf and brown gravy.

"We know you're helping at the library." Lucas put the glass of beer to his lips and took a sip. "We hoped maybe you could talk some sense into Alexander. No one else has been able to do it."

April placed her hands on the counter. "And what makes you think I can accomplish that?"

"If anyone can, it's you, Short Stuff." Lucas placed his hand on the back of her stool.

"I hate to sound Christmassy, but you're our last hope." Vince nodded.

"Last hope?" April's voice cracked as she brought her hand to her chest. "What do you mean?"

Lucas turned to face her and their knees brushed together. "The town is thinking of having a vote."

"A vote for what?" April whispered, and her face scrunched up as she tried to disappear into the barstool, away from Lucas's knees.

"Having him replaced," Vince stated.

April sat up straight. "But he's his own boss. He's the only one who can decide if he gets replaced. Not to mention the fact that the library is Alexander's entire life."

"We—the town—feels that if we can get the judge to back us up, we could finally have the changes we've all wanted. By way of a court order."

"That judge, she has a lot more power than anyone I know." April sighed. "Why would you do such a thing?" She looked at Vince and then Lucas, both avoided eye contact. "You *can't* do that to Alexander. He loves the library more than anything or anyone."

"Here ya go, hon!" Lillian's voice came through the kitchen's window as she slid a to-go bag on it, followed by a second one. "Could you be a dear and drop off Alexander's dinner also? I think his first day back at work was a bit more than he expected."

The waitress hurried behind the bar and handed April the bags. "Alexander already paid."

"Sure, it's on my way." April slapped a ten on the counter. "Keep the change."

"Think about what we said," Vince said over his shoulder.

April held both containers in her grip. "I will."

As she made her way out, Luis gave her a wave, and she spotted Trinity and Camden, who were in a corner booth with their daughter, adding a wave for them also.

Pushing open the door, the chill in the air tickled her cheeks. Maybe chatting with Alexander outside the library walls would be just what she needed to do. And this meal delivery was the perfect opportunity. April couldn't allow him to lose his true love.

Although as she traveled the quick two-minute drive back toward her parents' house, April knew she needed to grab something that might be helpful before she went to Alexander's house.

Chapter 16

Alexander

Alexander opened the front door to find April standing with two food containers. "Hi, how may I help you?"

April leaned back, confusion in her eyes. "You make me feel like a telemarketer."

"You're not on my phone."

She pinched her eyes shut and shook her head. "Do you mind if I come inside? I mixed up the containers, and I'm not sure which one is yours and which one is mine."

"Where's Frank?"

"I dropped him off at home. He was hungry and needed some downtime. And I know how much you love him."

"Oh." He stepped aside and allowed her to come in. "Don't say Luis sent you with my meal? I didn't mean to inconvenience you. I was going to pick it up." He glanced down. "Please excuse my attire."

After work, he'd taken a nice, long warm shower and dressed in more comfortable clothing. It was then he'd realized he was low on food and had zero energy to cook anything even if he had something to whip up. But Luis had offered to drive it over and there'd been no mention of April in the conversation.

"Nonsense, you always look put together." April waved him off using her elbow as she entered his trailer.

Alexander continued to glance down at his sock-covered feet and gray sweat bottoms while April placed the containers on the nearby kitchen counter and popped open one of the lids. "Oh, this is soup and fresh bread. It's mine."

"I believe it's mine. I ordered soup."

She looked at him, and warmth spread through him like the first sip of hot chocolate on cold lips. *Don't think about lips. Her lips. No one's lips, especially April's.*

"You ordered soup too?" She held one of the containers at eye level.

"Yes, cream of potato." He reached out his hand for it.

April smiled and tilted her head to the right, allowing espresso-colored ringlets to cascade over her shoulder. "That's what I got, how funny. I never would have thought we would like the same thing." She glanced at the container and then back at him. "Would you like some company for dinner?"

All the blood traveling through his veins flooded into his toes. *April. Here? Dinner together?* "I suspect that would be acceptable."

"Perfect. Why don't you have a seat, and I'll get our dinner served up." April spun towards the kitchen cabinets, and her dress twirled as though it belonged on a joyful child. "Where are your plates and bowls?"

Even the thought of someone else getting items from his kitchen was off-putting and un-host-like, but something about April made the experience acceptable. It was as though she belonged.

"Both are in the cupboard to the left of the stove." Alexander glanced at the kitchen table and then the couch. It was proper to sit at the table, especially with a guest over. But the pain in his back let him know sitting in the chair would be darn impossible.

"Are you alright if we eat in the living room?" April set the plates on the counter and added the bowls. "I'm sure it would be better for your back."

"Thank you, if you don't mind being informal."

April laughed, "I think informal is my middle name."

He let out a short huff of laughter, catching in his throat before it grew boastful.

"I don't know if I've ever heard you laugh before." She reached for her purse on the kitchen table. "I just so happen to have a Christmas movie if you'd like to watch it while we eat."

"Do you always carry movies in your purse?" Alexander lowered himself onto the couch and adjusted the pillows behind his back.

"Only when the occasion calls for it." April set his plate with bread and butter and soup bowl on the coffee table in front of him then laid a nearby pillow on his lap and moved the dishware, balancing it on top. "Do you need any salt? Pepper?"

"No, thank you. Lillian always makes it just right."

She hurried back to the kitchen. "I agree." When April returned, she set her plate and bowl on the coffee table next to him and paused. "Where is your DVD player?" She waved the movie in her hand.

"Behind the left door in the credenza. What movie are we going to watch?"

"*Home Alone.*" She kneeled, popped open the door, and turned on the player.

When she removed the disc from the case, he wanted to object, yet he also wanted to watch it. Everything inside him raged a little war of unexpected joy and happiness against the unknown and impossible. And when he thought back, he realized it'd been occurring since April appeared to help out at the library. He tried to shake the notion from his mind; clearly, it was due to the holiday season, although he'd celebrated many Christmases without this specific feeling since his mom passed. Alas, it could be the pain medications he was taking.

"Before you tell me no"—April was back to sitting on the couch a few feet from him when he came from his thoughts—"give it a chance."

A chance? "A chance?"

She blinked a few extra times and beamed a smile in his direction. "The movie, silly. It's one of my favorites. And I'm bending my tradition by eating soup while watching instead of a cheese pizza."

"Do you always eat pizza with movies?" Alexander blew on this spoon of soup.

"No, but I do with this one. You'll see why soon enough." April tore off a piece of the roll, and he watched as she set it on her tongue.

She peeked over at him. "Trust me."

A smile creased on his lips, and he nodded, infatuated with the current moment. Turning his attention to the television, he attempted not to look back over at the woman he found so beautiful. Since the first time he saw her in high school, he'd had a crush on her. Only now, as an adult, it felt like much more than that.

Chapter 17

April

April wondered if Alexander ever tired of being perfect. Maybe his quintessential life rules provided him with structure in a world of unknowns, but how did he ever have any fun? Yet, during *Home Alone*, she noticed he had the best laugh she'd ever heard. She even wondered if anyone in Woolsey had ever heard it before, outside of his father. It started low and vibrated into many deep huffs and made her think if a mountain could laugh, it would be as manly as Alexander's.

As she returned her focus to the movie, credits rolled up on the screen. April folded her right foot under her leg. Without a doubt, she could remain in that very spot for a long time. "Did you like it?"

Alexander rested his head on the pillows behind him and rolled it to the side, their eyes meeting for seconds before he finally spoke. "We must show this at the library."

"Really?" The unexpected agreement caused her to sit straight up.

"Yes. Truthfully, I feel this movie is far better than others nowadays. And I apologize for forming an opinion beforehand."

"You don't need to apologize. I've done the same thing when boyfriends would bring over movies."

"And you've had a lot of boyfriends with poor movie choices? Or have some of them been good surprises?"

The way Alexander spoke reminded her of a maître d' who double-checked that her truffle poached lobster was to her satisfaction.

"I've not had many boyfriends, more boy-*slash*-friends. Believe it or not, I'm not much of anyone's cup of tea. I'm my own person, and most men want me to be whatever they want, not what I want."

"And that caused *fewer* boyfriends? I find that trait hard to come by, especially in a person with your grandeur."

Warmth traveled from her heart to her fingertips and the tops of her cheeks. "I dress as though I enjoy five-star restaurants and all the fluffy little things men say to try and convince us women that they are the one. While it's nice, I'd rather bring food home and cuddle on the couch or share a book and chat about it over a homemade dinner. I'm too old-fashioned, too much of a homebody, for many of them. And the other ones, well, they never seem to notice me."

Alexander glanced back at the television as though it gave him a few extra seconds to keep from responding.

"When men discover I have anxiety in crowded situations—being out at a busy bar, hence why I ended

111

up with Frank—it allowed for plenty of first dates but never second ones. I mean, most couples love going out, they go to local fairs when they come to town, concerts, bustling restaurants. Just think, how boring would that *When Harry Met Sally* restaurant scene be if they were alone at home instead of out in public?"

"I've seen that movie. However, I'm certain your dates knew about Frank and his purpose?"

"Did you?" April felt her posture slump as Cora jumped off the top of the couch.

Alexander used the remote to lower the volume on the television but kept the movie's credits running. "I admit, not at first. For that I apologize, I've learned a lesson."

"I learned to watch what I judge, such as your friend-ship with Charlie."

Charlie and Alexander didn't seem like the most com-patible of friends. Until Alexander let the secret slip to April about how he was letting Charlie use the library's computer to chat with Desert Girl a few nights a week. Love was abloom as far as Alexander could determine.

"You promised not to mention anything about Charlie and his Desert Girl," he warned.

She shook her head and accidentally allowed her hand to reach out to his arm and patted it. "I did promise, and I stand by it, but *we* can talk about it."

Alexander's eyes lit up and reflected the white Christ-mas tree lights from the corner. "I do assume you're correct. But we should focus on the upcoming library celebration and showing *Home Alone*."

"We could do strings of fairy lights on the ceiling to make it look like a starry night." April rose from the couch and made a rainbow shape motion with her hands.

Alexander shifted on the couch and moved the pillows. "What else do you have in mind?"

April went to the Christmas tree, looked at the matching ornaments, and then twisted back toward the couch. "We need a new Christmas tree. Sorry, that's on me, but we'll decorate it together this time. What else do you typically do for the celebration? It's been so long since I last attended."

"We do a shortened reading of *A Christmas Carol*, draw Christmas scenes on paper, and of course, our buffet feast."

"And?" April approached the couch and sat back down.

"And, then they go home." Alex scratched at his hairline.

"No gingerbread house construction?"

"Sticky hands around all the books?" His eyebrows rose.

"No snowflake cutting?"

Alexander shook his head.

April crossed her arms. "I see your point; it is a small library with little room to move around without causing an issue. But what about doing it out in the hallway? The city center is pretty big, and it would still be a part of the celebration, even if not in the actual library."

"This sounds like it'll cost a lot. The library doesn't have much in the way of funds, and I can only allocate a small portion to the celebration every year."

April stood back up. Every second she sat next to Alexander, her hands wanted to reach out to touch his arm or hold his hand, and she couldn't have any of that. She was not staying in town, and she was not taking away Alexander's job.

Going to the living room window that overlooked the front of Alexander's property, she allowed a sigh to escape. "That brings me to the next point." She didn't turn around; she couldn't take whatever expression would come across his face. "The library needs a face-lift outside of the celebration."

She had no idea how he would take her confronting him with it but figured doing it after he was in a good mood from *Home Alone* might be her best shot.

A groan came from behind her, and fearful, she turned around to find Alexander pushing himself off the couch like a pregnant lady, holding his back with his hand. He went to the kitchen and grabbed a glass from the cupboard before pouring himself filtered water from the dispenser at the sink.

Alexander took a long gulp, and the sound of the glass being set on the counter seemed to vibrate in her heart. "You're trying to take my job from me. My library."

April shook her head and walked past a stretching Cora and into the kitchen. "No, I'm not."

"You know I'm the boss, the head boss. I can't fire myself."

"I never said anything about being fired."

"Not one resident has ever come into the library to tell me they want changes." Alexander gulped down the rest of his water and refilled it. "And come to think of it, not a single person set foot in there today. The hold shelf is overflowing, and if they wanted change, I'd have heard about it by now."

"People probably stayed away because I tried to set the library on fire first thing this morning." She giggled and saw he didn't feel the same way about the situation and covered her mouth.

April moved closer to him, and the urge to reach out to him caused her fingers to pulse at the tips as his hurt expression tugged at her heart. "I'm not a threat to your library or your job. I want to see the residents love to go there, and right now, they don't."

"How do you know they don't love the library? They check out books, don't they?" Alexander set the glass on the counter with a clink.

"They want to see you fix it, make it a little fresher, add some modern conveniences, or they plan to replace you with the help of the judge." She closed her eyes as the words hit Alexander. The last thing she wanted to do was see the disappointment on his face worsen. Her heart lurched as though it had been yanked out of her chest and now swung wildly from a string.

"You said it wasn't about me being fired."

April stood next to him at the sink, frozen.

The movie's credits had ended, and the DVD switched back to the main menu screen, causing a blanket of silence to cover the trailer. And the world around her seemed equally quiet, so much so that she thought it might be snowing outside for a second. That was something she loved about her time in Washington, the sound of the city when it snowed, right before everyone tried to venture out and the cars went slipping and sliding around. The moment when all things paused, and nature took over, hushing worries and spreading possibilities.

"Can you help me?" His voice broke through her imaginary snowstorm. "Will you help me?" Alexander focused on her like she was his last hope on Earth.

"Yes, of course." She rested her hands on the counter, noticing that Alexander's pinkie was a mere inch from her finger. "I'm not here to take the library away from you, I'm not staying, and I won't be getting a job here. I know how much you love the library, and the town sees it, too, but the residents need a happy medium."

"I don't understand why this sudden change is needed. There is absolutely nothing wrong with the library." Alexander lowered his head and shuffled out of the kitchen.

"It's not a sudden change. From what others are saying, they've wanted it for years now." April followed after him. "And you're right, there's nothing wrong with the library, but it's not all it can be, and it's not working for the residents anymore. The Christmas celebration will be the perfect opportunity to showcase the best one yet, present the proposed upgrades, and let the residents see you're willing to support the library's evolution with the times."

Alexander paused, and she nearly crashed into his back. Her hands jetted outwards as she stumbled to move to the side of him, grabbing for the edge of the couch.

He turned around as she rested her hand on the top of the couch, still warm from when Cora had curled up there during the movie. "The celebration is days away. There is no way we'll have time to get everything done, especially in my current condition."

"Please have some faith. It's the holidays."

Alexander never wanted her to be there in the first place. They were completely different people. He loved classics, and she loved sci-fi. He enjoyed starched button-down shirts and dress shoes. She enjoyed soft, comfortable attire.

"The library is my heart and home." The gentleness of his hand grazed her arm and pulled her from the negative opposite thoughts.

April's vision went to his hand on her arm, and then, without thinking clearly, lost in the spirit of the simple Christmas items around his living room, she moved her hand on top of his. "Then make the library feel as wonderful to others as it feels to you. And we'll do it together."

When she drew her head up, her vision met his, and all she could do was stare into his eyes. A vulnerability in his rain cloud gray irises came across as sad and worried. Which made wanting to kiss him at that moment highly inappropriate, but the urge remained.

"Frank probably misses you."

She blinked. "Uh." She glanced around, trying to re-gain her composure. "Right, I didn't mean to overstay my welcome. Not that I was even supposed to be here in the first place." April spotted her purse on the kitchen table. "I'm sorry to have disrupted your night." She flung the purse over her shoulder. "If you could bring *Home Alone* to work tomorrow . . ." Pausing as though she couldn't find the front door, April added, "We're showing it at the library, so it has to be there, anyway."

"April," Alexander said, taking several steps until he was directly in front of her. "You didn't ruin my evening. On the contrary, you made it a pleasant surprise."

The tension in her shoulders eased, and with it, the purse slid to the crook of her arm.

"I'd walk you home, as any gentleman should, but your car is out there." He slid his hands into his sweatpants pockets.

"I hope you enjoy the rest of your night, Alexander." She opened the front door, and the chill of night air tickled the skin on her bare arms.

"Wait, you don't have a jacket?" His fingertips grazed the goose bumps on her arm, making them rise even higher.

"Oh, I'm okay."

When she turned around to say good night, Alexander held an olive-colored cardigan. "I insist." He held it open for her to thread her arms into.

She turned around and, with his help, slid it on. "Thank you. I'll return it tomorrow. Good night, Alexander."

He leaned against the door frame. "Good night, April."

As she walked to her car, a gentle breeze swirled around, and the scent of vanilla and cedarwood from the sweater warmed her. A fragrance that would forever remind her of Alexander, and she hoped he didn't see her smile as she tucked her chin to inhale his scent on the collar.

Chapter 18

Alexander

Today would be a lot of work, physically, and that was being open-minded. However, Alexander was willing to give it his very best. He'd even gone as far as to dress less *himself*. Instead of a button-down, he went with a navy polo shirt, and while he still tucked it into his dress slacks, it was enough of a change that he gave himself points for effort.

Like every work morning, Alexander walked to the library, and his physical therapist said the walking was good for him. Approaching the city center parking lot, he spotted April's car and instantly grinned. Even though he couldn't see his face, he felt how goofy his smile must have looked and quickly straightened his lips.

Keith held open the city center's main door. "Good morning, Alexander."

"Good morning, Keith." Alexander stepped inside, feeling the strain under his eyes from lack of sleep last night.

Immediately, he spotted Frank and then April at the library door, trying to get the key into the lock. She wore a big red-and-green plaid skirt and an ivory long-sleeve blouse.

He cleared his throat. "Good morning, Frank and April."

At the sound of his voice, she spun around, and the key that was nearly in the lock crashed to the floor.

"I'd help you pick that up, but seeing as though it took me five minutes to get my socks on this morning . . ."

She beamed and reached down to swipe up the keys. "Rough night?" April pointed at his eyes as she unlocked the door.

"Is it obvious?"

"Only a lot." She half-smiled and unclipped Frank's leash. "Thanks for allowing him to keep coming with me."

"After giving it thought, not only do I apologize for being rude about Frank, but it seems harsh for a service dog to not be with its owner."

The dog waddled over to the blanket still lying next to the check-out desk and flopped down. April set her purse on the desk and removed a stuffed lamb. Frank nearly jumped to attention.

"Okay," April said, and the dog took it in his mouth and curled up into a ball with the lamb.

He put a hand on the small of his back and observed the library. "I have no idea where to start or even what I'm doing."

"That's why I'm here. Don't let me forget about Aurora's book club proposal." Her hand grazed his shoulder, and he did his best not to flinch. Alexander didn't expect it at all, but the comfort it brought, the unknown desire for her hand to remain, worried him as he nodded at her book club mention in a trance.

Today, April's hair was pulled back into a low ponytail and curled at the base. It appeared soft as butter, and he envisioned running his fingers through it.

"And I even made a list." She bumped her shoulder with his. "Aren't you proud of me?"

Always. "Yes, you've been a great help to the library. I should be upfront and tell you that even if I disagree, you being here has helped me see things I might not have otherwise been alerted to." He headed for the desk chair. "However, I already need to sit. I'm sorry, April, I don't know how much use I'll be."

"All you need to do is relax and open your mind to the suggestions. And if you don't, I'll sic Frank on you." She let out a laugh.

Alexander glanced down at Frank, who eyed him for a second before returning to try to destroy his lamb's right ear.

"I wanted to ask you more about Frank. I'm interested in attaining detailed information about the process regarding his assistance. I read a book on service dogs once, but firsthand knowledge is always a better account."

April dragged a chair opposite his desk and sat, crossing her legs with her notepad on top of her lap. "Really?"

"Yes, absolutely."

She rested her hands on top of the paper, pen in hand, and tilted her head. "I'd love that. But first, how do you feel about a puzzle table?"

"For a puzzle? What does that have to do with reading?"

"Book-inspired puzzles. You have all these empty tables for studying, which people are not using, especially without any computers."

"But they can bring their laptops." He glanced at a nearby table.

"You only have internet on your office computer and don't offer Wi-Fi."

He crossed his arms.

"So, literary-themed puzzles?"

"Fine." Alexander uncrossed his arms.

"Wonderful, I've located several online, and we can get them rather cheaply. Plus, they can be reused many times because not everyone will be working on them at once."

"I like the sound of that, with the literary theme. I bet they even have one with a compilation of the great American novels. Maybe we could have themed puzzles for the holidays, such as *A Christmas Carol,* and one for the children, like *How the Grinch Stole Christmas.*"

Alexander felt a surge of excitement, and much to his chagrin, he couldn't remember the last time he'd done a puzzle. He always enjoyed them, but oftentimes his parents' kitchen table was covered with his school books or dinner plates, and after he cracked his head on the coffee table as a toddler, his mom got rid of it and vowed to never have one in the house again. To this day, his father didn't own one either.

"Perfect, we'll put that on the list. Now let's think of some more projects we can do for the Christmas celebration. So far, I have the agreed-upon *Home Alone* with lights." She looked up from her list and scanned the room.

If only he'd gotten more sleep last night, he might be of more help today. He'd done his best not to think about April once his head hit the pillow. Instead, he'd turned his focus to the library and what he could possibly change to create a place where residents wanted to be without losing his job or his sanity.

"Change is not in my wheelhouse," he said.

"It's not." She laughed, and when she looked up, her face went solemn. "I mean, nonsense. You need to push your thinking out the doors. Open up, look around, get outside of your normal ideas." She closed her eyes and took a deep breath.

Alexander's vision froze as he stared at April, desiring to know what she was thinking, what she dreamed about. What her favorite book was, and if she loved mornings as much as he did. He couldn't pull his vision from her closed eyes, and when she opened them, he kept staring.

"Well?" April leaned forward.

"Sticky hands." He pressed his lips together, muffling a chuckle.

"Sticky . . . oh, gingerbread." She beamed. "Yes, in the hall, we can have the best of both worlds. Fun and sticky hands far from the pages of books. And you can make one, too."

He shook his head. "I'm not sure we should venture that far."

"We'll revisit it later." She crossed her legs the other way. "What else can we do for the library outside of Christmas?"

"You'd mentioned offering DVDs and matching them with a book, but I simply don't know how I feel about that."

"How about meeting halfway and ordering a few DVDs for a few popular books? And how about several audio books and a few e-books via a catalog subscription?"

Alexander crossed his arms. "I don't have those e-readers to check them out."

She giggled. "You don't need them. The patrons will have their own tablets, and they can check them out through the library database via Hoopla or other apps. It allows you to offer the newest releases without needing the extra shelf space or worrying about people damaging the books."

"I guess I still have a lot to learn." He felt himself drop into discouragement.

"Don't worry. Remember, I'm here to help." April winked.

He most certainly hadn't forgotten she was there; whether she was helping or hurting right now would remain to be seen. When the Christmas season was over, his back healed, and with April out of town, he'd find out just how much hurt she could cause. And he wasn't looking forward to it.

Alex looked out at the empty middle of the library. "What are the plans for the Christmas tree?"

"What if we get a tree but don't decorate it?" she suggested.

"Don't decorate it? How is not decorating it a theme?"

"Natural, it's a theme, no?" Her lips rose in the corners of her mouth.

Again, he found himself lost, staring at her mouth. He needed to get off the pain medication—it caused him to be completely erratic and infatuated. "It's a beautiful idea, April." He pressed his hands into the small of his back.

"Yay," she cheered, stomping her feet in little pitter-patters as she continued to make notes. "Since this year will be new and improved, I'll make up a flyer to post around town so everyone coming will know what to bring to the LCC."

"Indeed, we'll need a flyer."

"I think if we can get a few donations—or at least discounts from Charlie at the grocery store—this will work out rather well."

"Discounts? What do we need from the grocery store?"

"Snacks for the movie, supplies for the gingerbread houses." April continued to write on the notepad and didn't look up at him. "I'm excited, aren't you?"

He didn't want to spring up with joy, although it coursed through him like a sugar rush. "I do believe it should liven up the place."

"Come on, Alexander. 'Tis the season, and we're going to make the very best of it by showing this town what you and the library have to offer." She sprang up and went to a bookcase in the children's section.

"Just look at all these picture books." April slid a few from the shelves, flashing the Christmas-themed books in his direction. "Put these out on display, show the kids what they're missing."

"Books belong filed properly in a bookcase, not all willy-nilly out and about. That's how they get damaged."

"It's how they get read."

"You're a real Mary Poppins, you know that?" He felt like a kid around her, as though he could do anything, but they were adults, and he shouldn't feel like a kid around anyone.

"That's the best compliment anyone could give me." She twirled around with the books pulled tight to her chest.

At that moment, he wanted to pick her up and twirl around with her. Seeing as how his emotions were child-like and ridiculous at the moment, he could fully picture himself doing just that if not for his recent surgery.

"Now . . ." She approached his chair. "We need to discuss the office computer. Other than it being from the 1990s, the Internet signal is spotty across town, but here it's solid. And I think it's a good time to update the computer so you can switch out the Dewey decimal system for the BISAC system."

He blinked.

"Alexander, you know, the barcode scanning for check-out is a good thing."

Well, now she's being ridiculous.

Chapter 19

April

It bothered April that Christmas in Woolsey was missing something. It hadn't been an issue before she'd experienced the snowy coldness that she'd learned to love while in college. She'd never been big on snow, but after encountering the joy of it during the holiday season, she felt the ache in her soul. April loved to watch snowflakes fall from the silver clouds during walks with Frank as they covered Christmas lights strung over porch decks.

Yet, the desert had its own Christmas magic, and she was determined to capture it after the last few years of being without it. And not only did she need to do this for herself, but for the library as well.

Taking a peek out the living room window, April was happy to see a cloudy day. The blue sky was completely hidden, for once. She continued to stare as her vision blurred, deep in thought.

Sure, the decorations made everything feel Christmassy once the curtains and blinds were closed. And while she loved the desert, she longed to feel the wintry magic. So, in order to do that, she had to dig deep into what she could do to bring in something special, something unexpected.

"Snow!" April nearly leaped off the couch. "How can I get snow?"

She thought of only one answer, the school. Picking up her phone, she searched for Sherri, the principal at Woolsey Elementary. However, the last time Sherri had spoken with her was at the annual Halloween party before she left for college, and she wasn't big on calling someone up out of the blue to ask for a favor.

The line picked up. "Hello?"

"Sherri, it's April Gardner."

"Hi, April. How are you? How are your parents?"

"I'm great, as are they . . . wherever they're at the moment. I do hate calling simply to ask a favor, but . . ."

"April, you're no longer a pupil at my school. Whatcha got?"

April clicked on the stove's burner where the tea kettle sat. "I'm working with Alexander at the library, and we wanted to do something special this year for the Christmas celebration. I'd like to surprise Alexander, if possible." She removed a Santa mug from the cupboard. "I had an idea to bring snow in for the kids, but we need someplace bigger and safer than the parking lot of the city center."

"The schoolyard would be a perfect spot," Sherri stated. "But I must ask, how will you possibly pay for it?"

April dug through her parents' tea stash, looking for the lavender chamomile. "I was hoping maybe we could split it with the school." She dropped the tea bag in the top of Santa's head. "If we get it delivered to the schoolyard, we could share it with the school kids the day after."

"Won't it melt by the next day?"

"I checked the temperatures forecasted for the day of the Library's Christmas Celebration, and the high is showing in the fifties with an overnight low in mid-thirties." April picked up the tea kettle just before it let out its whistle. "If we get the snow placed in the grass area to the north of the building, it will block the sun from reaching it in the afternoon. Which means if it's the last activity before the movie and feast at the celebration, it would be dropped off later in the day. In the morning, the kids can play with it during recess before it warms up and melts."

The line was silent. "Alright, we'll split the cost; the school has the funds. Email me the payment details, and we'll get it set up."

"Thanks so much, Sherri."

"You're welcome. Be sure and tell your parents I said hi."

After ending the call and steeping the tea, April took the mug to the living room and opened up her laptop.

"Time to write up the flyers," she said to Frank as she sat next to him on the couch.

Before she opened the document, April checked her email and spotted an unread message from the Washington State Law Library in Olympia. She'd applied for a position there right before her graduation from the university and hadn't necessarily forgotten about it but assumed it was a pass since she didn't hear back by the deadline.

"Oh my goodness!" She covered her mouth and read through the email. "They want to interview me."

April reread the email and noticed the date of the interview request was for this coming Sunday, the same day as the Library's Christmas Celebration.

"Who does an interview on a Sunday?" Her hand found the top of Frank, and she began to pet him. She kept reading, fearing she'd have to be on a plane without any notice, but with further reading, she discovered it would be an online video interview since they knew she was currently out of state. Wrapping both hands around the warmth of the mug, she leaned back into the couch.

The interview time was for three in the afternoon. However, that would be four here since Washington was on Pacific Standard Time and Arizona was on Mountain Standard Time. While she could sneak off and use her laptop, the timing would pull her away from the celebration. She could easily use the break room in the city center, but the likelihood that it would be quiet enough, even with the door closed, would be doubtful with the gingerbread station in the hall.

"There's no way I can ask to postpone the interview, and I certainly can't turn it down." With her mug, she paced the living room, telling her worries to Frank. "I'll talk to Alexander and let him know that I need to slip away for a short time."

The bulldog stood on the couch, shook, and then moved from his spot to the left side and flopped down next to a throw pillow.

"I'll inform Alexander that I have an interview. He'll be happy for me. It's not like I'm staying. I can't stay, there simply isn't enough room in town for the both of us. He wants his job back full-time." However, the more she thought about it, the less confident she felt. Happy or not, Alexander would need her help until his back was one hundred percent again.

She opened the slider and went out onto the patio with her tea. The chill in the air made her shiver, causing her to bring her knees to her chest once she sat in the patio chair.

Typically, April would instantly be daydreaming about landing the position and envisioning her life in Washington. She'd spent a lot of time in the Seattle area while at the university, with her and Frank traveling up and down the I-5 exploring little towns like Edmonds and the fancy neighborhoods of Bellevue, Anacortes, and Camano Island. It was very different from life in the desert and living there full time was not something she put much thought into, even when applying for the job.

To be honest, she'd not thought much about where she wanted to settle down once she graduated. The fact that her parents could RV wherever she lived helped ease her worries about how often she'd see them. Before April left for college, she was willing to explore any area until she stepped foot in the big city and was unexpectantly crippled with anxiety. With Frank's presence, she was hopeful that he would help her navigate any roadblocks that prevented her from following her future career goals. She wanted to work in a beautifully enormous library, one historically overwhelming with books.

The professor for her final two classes had recommended she apply for the open spot in Olympia, and while she had, April also knew it was a long shot, regardless of her anxiety. The letter of reference she attached to her application must've had more pull than she thought.

April set her mug on the dusty patio table and wrapped herself tighter in her heather gray cardigan sweater as the air grew with moisture. The cozy fabric was soft against her fingers. If she remembered correctly, before they left for their current trip, her parents had said the last time it rained was two months ago. While she hadn't grown up in Woolsey, it was her home, at least since her teenage years. But there was no future here. She'd known coming home to reside in the little town after graduation would be short-lived.

If she wanted to stay in the state and utilize her degree, her only choice would require moving to Phoenix or Tucson, someplace with enough opportunity for employment. Once the new year arrived, she'd planned to apply for everything possible, with Frank a part of the résumé.

But now, something about Woolsey felt different, and it wasn't simply the winter air. Just as Alexander's face popped into her mind, a familiar face matching many of his features came into her line of sight.

"William?" April stood from the chair as the distant snore of Frank on the couch drifted out of the slider's screen.

"Little April, do you have a spare moment?"

His gait was stable, but he appeared to be heading to the right of the patio, and she was on the left.

"William." She gave a wave as though to redirect him. "I have more than a moment for you. I have at least three."

"Little April, you spoil me." William lifted the brim of his veteran's cap.

She motioned to a patio chair. "Can I get you something to drink? I'm having tea." April lifted her mug in his direction.

"No, thank you. I enjoyed a meal with Lillian at the diner." He felt for the chair and then eased into it, and April sank back into the one she'd been occupying.

"Oh?"

"I received some interesting information."

April leaned toward Alexander's dad, and a little bit of her hoped the information was about his son. "I always enjoy information."

"I shouldn't say anything, but ever since I was forced to retire from the city center, I've missed being in the center of everything. Literally, mind you." He chuckled, and it reminded her of Alexander's mountainous laugh. "Lillian is seeing someone."

"Someone?" April brought the mug to her lips.

"She won't say because she can't." William glanced around as though he'd been followed. "He's . . . online."

135

She nodded her head as though hearing the gossip for the first time. "Online? Well, William, I think many people meet online nowadays."

William leaned back into the chair and brought his hands together in the shape of a tent. "Yes, but usually they know who they're speaking with—a name, a face, something. Yet, Lillian doesn't know anything about this man other than he goes by Desert Guy."

April choked on her tea and covered her mouth as she coughed.

"Are you alright, Little April?" William asked, his hands lowering to his lap.

Raindrops, big and full of coldness, fell from the sky, plopping against the undisturbed dust.

She cleared her throat as the water continued its downpour, sounding like marbles hitting the earth. "Desert Guy? Do you happen to know what name Lillian uses?"

"Lillian goes by Desert Girl. How coincidental is that?" William asked over the sound of the intensifying storm.

April could only nod, knowing the secret that no one else knew, not even Alexander—he only knew half of the mystery.

"Let's get you home before we're soaked to the bone." April set her mug down. It was already full of extra water and dust, and guided William towards his trailer.

Who would've thought sleepy ole Woolsey had a saucy love story?

Chapter 20

Alexander

Alexander lay in bed, unable to fall back asleep. The sound of rain continued to hit the siding and roof of his trailer. Usually, he'd be at the window, admiring the rain like a child with delight coursing through him. That was what happened to almost everyone who lived in the desert when it rained—it was like watching the Rockefeller tree go up once a year.

Every time he closed his eyes, images from *Home Alone* replayed in his memory, creating a smile to form on his face as he remembered scenes that caused him to chuckle.

He couldn't wait to show the movie at the library. Something about the joy of Christmas was getting to him this year. It was good, but it was something he was not familiar with. Even as a child, Christmas was a holiday where his mom was the reason it was joyful. Sure, they enjoyed classic movies, but what made it Christmas were the small things his mom did for him. She'd hide chocolate coins in his backpack or leave one on his dresser to find in the morning. She'd tie elaborate green and red bows around wrapped items he already owned as a way to add decorations to his room. When he'd come home from school, his mom would be humming a Christmas carol and baking with her Mrs. Claus apron on.

He thought of his father decorating the outside of the trailer in lights and hanging a wreath on the door. The way he watched his parents dance together in the living room to "Rockin' Around the Christmas Tree." But once his mom passed away, Christmas became a memory of all the things he missed about her and how she loved the season, making it more than a holiday. And doing any of the things his mom had done caused guilt to fill him because he knew he could never bring the type of joy she did to Christmas.

Moving his feet over the side of the bed, he sat up. The pain in his lower back was less, and the throbbing sensation had reduced by at least half. He checked the time on his night table clock—4:35 a.m. Pausing, he looked out his bedroom window, low enough to see his father's trailer without having to move. The trailer that he had so many wonderful holiday memories celebrating with his parents. And even in the rain, he could see all his dad had up was a single strand of lights around the overhang.

He shook his head and lowered it, focusing on the tops of his pajama-covered thighs. He knew the rush of joy he felt when he was around April meant only one thing, and he needed to ignore those notions. April was like a cup of peppermint cocoa on Christmas Eve, and just like the holiday, she'd be gone by the new year. Soon, Woolsey would return to its normal ways—including the library and including his life. Not only were they complete opposites of each other in many ways, but Woolsey only had room for one librarian.

As he made his way down the short hall and into the living room, he went over and flipped on the Christmas tree's lights, something he only did when it was evening and the sun had set. Then, he poured water into a mug and heated it in the microwave. Within a minute thirty, he had a lovely hot chocolate and turned on his television.

Alexander opened up a streaming service app he'd recently uploaded, something else he had never done before but found it relatively easy. Too easy. And he saw why people could spend hours in front of the television instead of with their noses in a book. He browsed the Christmas movie section and noticed a popular movie he knew of but never watched, *National Lampoon's Christmas Vacation*.

Curiosity got the best of him, undoubtedly caused by the slippery slope that April had created with her joy of trying new things and the Christmas spirit. He checked the time on his cell phone sitting on the edge of the coffee table, 4:42 a.m. He'd been up early before when he did his morning run from his place to the gas station at the edge of town and back, a two-and-a-half-mile jaunt round trip. Yet, never this early, as he didn't usually lace up until 6 a.m. And with the start of his back pain, he'd put off running for over a year now. He wiggled his toes, thinking about how much he missed it.

Snatching his phone off the table, he located April in his contact list and stared at the tiny circle with an A. He wished he'd asked for a picture to use as her profile avatar, but it seemed juvenile. Alexander didn't have one for any of his contacts, not even his father. He felt if you needed a picture to go with a name, then maybe you didn't know the person well enough to call them up for a conversation.

If Alexander closed his eyes, he could see April—her smile, her everything. He could describe her to an artist, and they'd paint the most accurate portrait of her. Of course, he'd had girlfriends in the past, but only a few. His personality didn't mix with most of the girls he'd gone to school with, and he never went to college to explore that avenue. The girls in high school always deemed him as straightlaced and no fun. If they had a section in the yearbook his senior year for *tattletale*, his picture would've been under it.

In fact, he could often be found at the city center after school when his other classmates were hanging out in the grassy field behind the gym or loitering outside of the Shop and Save. Alexander had helped at the library as far back as he could recall. When his mom decided she wanted to retire, she picked Alexander as his replacement with a three-question, ten-second interview. While the timing was suspicious (the day after high school graduation), and of course, he was her son, Alexander was thrilled and he didn't care how dubious it seemed to everyone in town. He loved his job and was intelligent enough to know that he didn't have the college education required to work at any other library. His parents couldn't afford the cost of community college, never mind Arizona State University. And even with the best of jobs, the price would put him forever in debt. For a short while, he pondered the notion of taking out a student loan. Deep down inside, he knew he'd never leave Woolsey, and therefore he'd always be the town's librarian—until April threw a possible wrench into his future and residents speaking up about their desire for change.

Alexander understood he would be stuck in Woolsey forever, and that wasn't abysmal, but it wasn't a marvelous thing either. As long as he was satisfied with being a bachelor for the rest of his life. Nevertheless, he accepted his lot in life, and until April returned, he never gave it much thought. Even in the small senior class size, April and Alexander hadn't talked much. They had a few group projects together during their junior year and one in their senior year, but he was such a perfectionist that he did most of the work for the group himself. Therefore, getting to know any of his classmates outside of school was limited.

Cora stretched and let out a meow on the other side of the couch, and he refreshed his phone's screen, allowing April's contact information to return to life. Without realizing it, Alexander hit send.

"Hey, Alexander," she answered.

His upper body stiffened as he put the phone to his ear. Had he just called her at five in the morning? Alexander scrunched his nose, and his lips curled as though he'd sucked on a lime. "Hi, April. How are you?"

"I'm good," she drew out, her voice raspy. "Is everything okay?"

His eyes darted around the room. "Um." He never said *um*; although it was in the dictionary, he still didn't consider it a real word. "I didn't mean to disturb you this early."

"Are you alright?" Concern freckled her voice. "Do you need something? Is something wrong with your back?"

"Yes." *No.* He panicked, pushing himself up off the couch. "Yes. I mean, my back is fine. I was thinking about the library's celebration."

"Do you always wake up with library thoughts?"

He took a slurp of his hot chocolate. "I apologize for this call being early."

"No problem at all. To be honest, I've not been sleeping too well lately, so I've been up taking walks with Frank before the sun comes up."

"That's a shame about you not sleeping well. I used to love going for morning jogs myself."

"I hope you can get back to running when you're healed." There was silence, and then . . . "Did you need something?"

"It's silly, my sincerest apologies."

"Tell me." Her voice was sweet and soft, like a marshmallow warmed by hot chocolate. He picked up his mug and stared at it. "Hello? Alexander?"

"I was about to start watching *National Lamp*—"

"Yes!"

The phone picked up the sound of things moving around. "Yes?" And he held back a chuckle as the excitement built inside of him.

"Yes, I'll come over to watch *Christmas Vacation* with you. Can I bring anything?"

Alexander didn't know how to respond. Usually, when a date happened, he would be the proper gentleman and have everything planned. He'd pick up the woman and take her to dinner, which always involved a long drive to the nearest restaurant in the next town. And he was most certainly not in his pajamas, and the sun was up or at least setting, not rising. This was not proper, and he'd never been more informal in his life.

He ran his hand through his bed-squished hair. "I can honestly say I don't know."

"Give me ten, and I'll be at your door. Bye."

And with that, the call dropped. He said bye even though she'd already hung up. Then Alexander took a quick inventory of the trailer's living room. Clean, as always, which meant all he had to worry about was himself. However, he needed to be a proper host, so he hurried past Cora, into the kitchen to check on what he had to offer April.

He forgot about any pain that radiated in his back from his body's fast movements as he opened the cupboards. It was then he realized that his cupboards were as bare as the three bears'. The strand of Christmas lights out his kitchen window caught his eye.

"Dad." He checked the time on the stove. Thankfully, his old man would be up, drinking coffee and watching *Match Game* and *Password* reruns.

Alexander didn't bother putting on his jacket as he went out his slider, down the two steps into the backyard, and made his way over to his father's trailer. The rain had done a number to the dry landscape, causing his slippers to sink with each step as the rain, still heavy, soaked his shirt. There was a chill in the air coming from the rain, and it caused him to smile. Mixing with the Christmas lights, something about the desert made it feel like the traditional holiday season, even if there was zero snow to be had.

He rapped his fist on his father's back slider with rain running down his knuckles. The curtains were open, and he could see William relaxing in his recliner facing the television.

William turned toward the slider, and his face gave way that he was indeed not expecting to see anyone, let alone his son. He squinted and made a sour face.

"Alex?" he saw his father mouth.

Alexander waved like a three-year-old spotting Santa and wiggled the door handle, causing the slider to ease open. "Dad, I thought I told you to lock this." Alexander wiped his slippers as much as possible and entered.

"But then you can't come in whenever you need."

"I have a key," Alexander reminded him, heading straight for the kitchen.

"Right, well, what brings you by at this early hour?" William kicked his recliner footrest into place and stood up, pausing before taking a few unsteady steps.

"Do you have any—?" Alexander brought his hands to his hips. "I don't know what to serve at this hour."

"This I must hear." William made his way into the kitchen behind his son.

"April is on her way over. We're going to watch *National Lampoon's Christmas Vacation*. I found it on one of those streaming movie apps."

"Great one, a classic in my book. So you have a date? A morning date?"

"Can it be considered a date if it's in the morning?" Alexander knew precisely where his father kept everything in the kitchen since, usually, he helped his father unload his groceries. "I think I saw you bought those fake-fruit-filled pockets the last time I put away your food."

"You did."

"Women like those, right? Do you have any fruit? Bread for toast? Jelly? I'll restock whatever I take tonight after work."

"How many Little Aprils are coming over?" William leaned against the counter, moving his hands to his pockets.

"Why? Do you believe that's overkill on the food?" Alexander snatched a reusable bag from the drawer and filled it with the supplies. "We're two colleagues meeting up to watch a Christmas movie. It's not a date, or a crime, Dad."

"I think a crime is about to happen." William shuffled back and picked up his coffee mug.

"What crime, Dad?" Alexander hurried back to the slider cradling the bag.

"My son's heart is being stolen." William brought his mug to the middle of his chest.

Alexander froze mid-step. "Now you're being preposterous. Lock up."

William followed his son. "You're confusing the word *preposterous* with *correct*."

Alexander let out a gruff as he made his way back across the yard. Yet, in the stillness of the December rain, Alexander smiled as he heard his father's slider shut and lock. Frankly, he didn't care what this morning was labeled; he was just happy to be spending time with April.

Chapter 21

Alexander

"Your dad waved at me as I passed by." April stood at the door in a paw print flannel pajama set covered with an open-front cardigan sweater in heather gray. "At least, I think he did. I'm not sure if he could see who I was."

"He's spying on me." Alexander stepped aside as Cora dashed by with a meow. "Please come in."

She wiped her shoes back and forth on the front door mat. "He did have this silly grin." April's hair was twisted up into a clip near the crown of her head and damp from the rain.

"How do you know my father has dentures?"

"When I waitressed at the diner, he'd comment on how much he loved Lillian's meatloaf but how he often got his dentures stuck in it." She set a foiled-covered plate on the corner of his kitchen counter as the water from the rain ran off it.

Alexander shook his head. "That's information no one should have to hear."

April giggled and brought her cardigan together in the middle. "Sorry, I probably should've gotten dressed. I honestly didn't think about it until I put my shoes on, and by then, it was too late to bother."

"Good thing I didn't bother either." Alexander glanced down at his attire. "I hope Frank is okay being left behind."

"He is. He sleeps well during rainstorms from all those years in Washington." April raised the corner of the foil to display a plate of bacon. "I brought over the only thing I had on hand for breakfast. It's cold, but we can reheat it. I just made it last night when my stomach was giving me angry hunger pains."

"I think it will go great with the little bit I have to offer. I do apologize. I wasn't expecting company."

"I think it will be perfect no matter what." April waved him off, removed the foil, and set the plate into the microwave. "You seem to be moving around better. Is your back doing well?"

"Yes, I woke up and, for the first time, didn't have the stiffness. Physical therapy is helping and getting the rest I need, thanks to you." Alexander removed two plates from the cupboard. "But this rain—the moisture finds its way into your joints."

"It does indeed. And it's been my pleasure helping at the library. Although I miss your dad greeting me."

"You don't like Keith?"

"It's not that. Your dad never made me feel as though his eyes were glued to me."

"Is Keith being inappropriate? If so, I can speak with him."

She huffed a laugh. "No, he's fine actually. It's been Lucas trying to get me to go on a date with him. I'm always turning him down, but he's persistent. I don't know why he's trying so hard, we didn't get along in high school, that's why we broke up." April turned to him and folded her arms over her chest. "I'm sorry it's a stupid conversation. It doesn't matter, especially at this hour."

He had to know more. It was his competition. *No. April is not staying in Woolsey. Lucas isn't her type, and neither are you. Move on!*

"It's a shame when a person can't take a hint that someone is not interested." Alexander set a serving spoon into the bowl of cut oranges, bananas, and apples.

"You know what would be good?" April pointed at the bowl.

"If this had strawberries?"

"You're so cute, but no, a little whipped cream."

His cheeks instantly felt as rosy as a pink lady apple. The microwave beeped, and Alexander popped open the door and reached inside. Unexpectantly, the plate was hot to the touch, and he let out a yelp as he jerked his hand out of the microwave.

"Oh no!" April extended her hand to his and cupped it as she directed it to the sink. "I should've warned you that the plate gets darn hot in the microwave."

He didn't know if the lightheadedness came from the scorching feeling on his fingertips or from her hand wrapped around his. The frigid water tingled as it ran over his fingers. April smelled of honeysuckle and warm marshmallows, causing him to instinctually lean toward her and close his eyes.

"Alexander? Alex?"

He opened his eyes. Seeing her caused him to confuse if he was daydreaming or awake.

"Is there a reason no one calls you Alex?" April asked, her hand still holding his under the running water.

"It's not for me. Too informal, too personal."

"So your dad calls you Alex?"

He stood up straight as she let go of his hand, and he shut off the water. "No, he doesn't."

Alexander had not given his name any thought other than never having anyone call him Alex, not in school, not on dates, not in conversations. But April mentioning it, the way she'd said *Alex* caused him to crave it. He ached for her to say his name, in any form possible, even the informal one.

"Do you think I should be called Alex?"

"I think you should go with whatever you want." April backed away from the sink.

Silence and distance sprouted between them like a visible entity. He'd never before desired to kiss a woman as much as he did right then. Every ache and pain on his fingers and back disappeared, except the one that grew in his heart. *Change the subject. Get your head on straight.* "I heard from Charlie. The cactus on the mountain, the decorated one, his Internet lady wants to meet him there for the reveal. So she's clearly local or at least knows about the cactus tradition."

"'The reveal'?" April spooned fruit onto her plate along with two pieces of bacon and an untoasted fruit pastry, then snorted a laugh. "Is that not what it's called?"

"I'd think it would be called a date. And I'm pretty sure I know who the mystery Internet lady is, but I'm not telling."

"Oh." He frowned, feeling out of place that he didn't know something she did. "Wouldn't you like to heat that?" Alexander pointed at the fruit pastry. "We can toast it."

She held her plate up off the counter. "I actually like these untoasted."

"Me too. I thought I was the only one."

April smiled, and he swore his breathing halted long enough that he nearly choked when he inhaled again.

"So, what'll happen with Charlie's date?" April held up the coffee craft.

"A mug, that would be helpful to pour the coffee into." Alexander moved to the upper cupboard and pulled down one of his solid-black mugs from his matching set of four.

She took it from him—without their fingers touching—and poured herself a cup of steaming black liquid.

"Can I offer you any creamer?"

April shook her head. "I think today I'll take it black."

As they made their way to the couch together, April eased onto the cushion as she set her mug and plate on the coffee table. "I must admit, a first date on a mountain? I sure hope it goes well—that could end up poorly." She motioned and clapped her hands together. "Splat."

"That's a horrible thought." Alexander sat on the other side of the couch.

"But it's a thought." April took a sip of coffee. "I mean, if not that, there are a lot of chollas up there. It wouldn't take much to injure a person." Alexander leaned away from April. "Sorry." She lowered the mug from her lips. "I've been reading a plethora of murder mystery novels lately."

"Remind me to recommend several humorous novels for you next."

April reached out and grazed her hand on his arm as she smiled. "Thank you. And tell me what else you know about this date."

"Charlie's been asking to use the library's Internet for some time now, maybe even a few years. The in-person date is long overdue. I don't think he has anything to worry about murder-wise."

"When was the last time you were on a date?" April poked the fork into an apple slice. "Never mind, that's not any of my business."

"I don't mind. It's been a couple of years." He lifted the remote and directed it toward the television to hit start on the movie. "I'm sure you're on a date every weekend."

"Well, that sounds rather presumptuous."

Maybe it was all the moments they'd had prior. The pauses, the breathlessness, the infatuation and desire, but it rolled off his tongue before he could stop it.

"You're like that of a best-selling book—too beautiful inside and out for anyone to say no to."

National Lampoon's Christmas Vacation began playing on the television, and Alexander peeked over at April without moving his head. He spotted her blushing as she did her best not to look his way by focusing on the breakfast in front of her. Turning his vision back to the TV, he watched the opening credits. "I didn't know this was a cartoon?"

April covered her mouth as she giggled. And when she glanced over at him, he realized he could watch an avocado sprout and be happy as long as she was with him.

Chapter 22

April

April held her nose over her coffee cup later that morning. The sharp aroma of caramel helped her eyes to stay open as Alex entered the library.

"Are you late?" she asked, peeking up at the clock before putting her lips to her mug.

Alexander pushed his sleeve back and checked his watch. "My apologies, but I believe I was entertaining a coworker with Christmassy delight during the early hours of the morning."

"Did you use *Christmas* as an adjective? How very unlike Alexander." She smiled and gave Frank, who sat at her feet, a pet. "We should blame Clark Griswold."

He looked so cute, all tired and his hair not in its perfect form. She leaned farther over the counter. Had he not shaved? She could swear she saw a hint of stubble.

"Maybe I should have some more coffee." Alexander passed her and slumped into a chair. "Although I've already had my cup for the day."

April swallowed quickly to prevent her from choking on her coffee. "You mean to tell me you only have *one* cup of coffee a day? How do you function?"

"I go to bed before I'm tired. It allows for adequate sleep, thus preventing the need to rely on caffeine."

"That sounds horrible." April made her way over to him and sat down. She handed her mug to him. "Here, try a little. It's my special blend."

Alex eyed the mug, then her, then the mug again. Finally, he reached his hand out and took hold of it, causing their fingers to graze. *Stop touching his fingers, this isn't a romance novel!* The tips of his fingers rested on top of hers, and all her blood ran to them, each fingertip pulsing with its own heartbeat. Seconds passed, and neither of them moved, frozen in the transfer of a hot beverage.

"There you both are!" William declared.

She released her grip on the mug as Alexander took it, and they turned towards the door.

"Is everything alright, Dad?" he asked.

"I wanted to make sure everything was okay with you, son. And good morning, Little April."

"Good morning, William."

"I need to know what time my ham should be ready for the Library's Christmas Celebration. That judge has been pestering me." William lifted his veteran's hat and glanced around. "She's been offering to help."

"I don't think she means to bug you, Dad, she's excited. The town is looking forward to your cooking."

"Everyone really is," April confirmed.

"How was your date this morning?" William wiggled the hat back down.

"Dad," Alexander exhorted and stood up, handing April her mug. "It was not a date."

"We did have food and a movie." She took a sip of coffee, standing next to him. "I guess it was kind of a date."

William grinned at Alexander. "Finally, someone got him to watch it."

"'Classics' are *White Christmas*, *A Christmas Story*"—Alexander straightened a stack of flyers for the celebration on the corner of his desk and ran his fingers over the small aloe plant—"*It's a Wonderful Life.*"

"Anything you watch every holiday season is a classic," she said.

Alexander raised his pointer finger in the air. "By definition, that's a tradition."

April peered down at the top of her mug and rubbed her thumb against the edge. "They're both adjectives," she mumbled.

"I must correct you. Tradition is a noun. The other forms of it, traditionally, traditional, traditionalism, are adjectives."

April held up her hand. "I got it. I'm wrong, you're right."

Alexander clasped his hands together and glanced away for a second. "Dad, the ham needs to be ready to serve at about five. It will allow everyone time to eat after all the activities and while watching the movie."

She approached the desk and lowered herself onto the floor next to Frank. "I'm afraid I'll be busy at four, and the snow play will probably run well into the five o'clock hour. So Alexander will have to start up the potluck."

"Snow play?" Alexander adjusted his tie near his Adam's apple. "What snow?"

She craned her neck up and squinted at the fluorescent lights encasing Alexander's face. "I've arranged for snow to be brought in and set up on the elementary school's field. Surprise!"

"But that's not a tradition for the library's celebration." Alexander crossed his arms over his chest.

"The town's buzzing with joy already, and now snow! Little April has brought a fresh perspective to the library, and we're all excited for the Christmas celebration." William looked around. "And I hope she continues to be a part of the revitalization."

"We have so much left to do, including a replacement tree." She pointed at the empty Christmas tree stand behind them at the office's door. Yet, her mind was not focused on the library or even Christmas. Instead, all she could think about was her upcoming interview.

"Don't set this one on fire." William removed a pair of mismatched gloves from his coat pocket. "That's a different kind of spirit than Woolsey can handle." William winked and slowly turned around. "I'll let you kids get to it. In two days, we feast at five, it sounds like?"

"Yes, Dad, five."

And with that, Alexander's dad shuffle-stepped out of the library and into the city center's main hall.

"Do you want to . . ." Alexander stumbled with his words. "I mean, I know we have a lot to do, and maybe you're tired of me, but I have yet to watch *A White Christmas* this year. I could cook, and we could make a night of it."

"I can't." April shoved her mug to her lips so quickly that she hit her front teeth.

Shock splattered over his face.

April pressed her fingers to her lips and closed her eyes with the pain. "Sorry, I didn't mean it like that." She reached a hand toward him but didn't make contact. "I can't let you cook *and* host. Your back is still on the mend, and I crashed your place this morning. Let's do it at my parents'. I'll cook, and you bring over the movie."

He smiled like a kid on Christmas morning. "That would be swell, thank you."

Swell? Okay, Dennis the Menace. April pulled her upper lip down with her bottom lip to avoid the giggling. "But only if you're still feeling up to it. Today's going to be busy." She removed the notepad from her purse. "We need to get a new tree, and *I* need to *not* set it on fire. And we should add some more decorations all around the library."

"I must make a run to Cactus City, so why don't I pick up the tree?"

"That's too much work for you, especially with your back."

He placed his hand on it. "It's feeling much better today. I should be fine."

April knew enough stubborn men to know there was no point in arguing. "Then I'll work on decorations here. I think there are still some lights in the back, and I can string them on the ceiling."

"Yes, two sets of clear lights are on the shelf." He ran his hand over his chin. "I'd better head out."

The space between them didn't feel the same as it had earlier that morning. When they were watching the movie, she'd caught him stealing glances her way, especially during lines that they shared a laugh over. Maybe Alexander hadn't enjoyed their time as much as she had. She knew he couldn't be worried about her taking his job; even if she didn't land the interview on Sunday, she was leaving. She just didn't know where she could go. Woolsey was home, always.

April wanted to spend what time she had left in Woolsey with Alexander. And she couldn't recall the last time she'd desired to spend every minute with a man. "Call me if you run into any trouble. I'll be here."

"Thank you. I'll be back as soon as I can."

As she had this morning, she fought the urge not to hug him before they parted. The pull to put her arms around him and feel his warmth against her was more overwhelming than she expected. Instead, she gulped coffee and sighed. The space needed more than Christmas lights and a tree. It required something magical. And not something she found magical, as that had already gone poorly, but something that Alexander found magical.

April located the lights and a step stool. She climbed and hooked the first set of string lights in the corner, stopping only to take sips of her coffee before it grew cold. She'd need to let the lights drape and meet up in the center directly above the circle of chairs in the middle of the room. But with only two sets, she'd need more.

"Do you need a hand?"

April stepped down to find the judge standing next to the ladder. "Thanks, Elizabeth. I was thinking I'm going to need a lot more lights."

"That's what I was hoping you'd say. I was digging through storage in the courtroom, and found two old boxes of Christmas stuff, though I have no idea what's inside them."

"You don't need them?"

"I don't think there are enough Christmas lights in the world to make the courtroom festive." She sighed a groan. "They're back in my office."

"Do you know who they belong to?" April set her mug on the desk on the way out and followed Elizabeth to the courtroom.

"Rumor has it they belonged to Alexander's mom." The judge opened a door at the back of her office.

"That's right! She used to be the librarian. And the library was always so festive with her in charge."

The judge hoisted a box big enough that her chin rested on its top. April grabbed the other box labeled

Xmas, and she nearly jogged back to the library with the excitement of what was inside.

Setting the boxes side by side on the floor where the new Christmas tree would go, they pulled the tape off and eased back the cardboard lids. It was as near to a Christmas time capsule as she'd ever seen in any antique store. Classic C9 Christmas lights were neatly wrapped next to a stack of paper snowflakes and bingo cards. Small boxes held glass ornaments in crimson red and gold. At the bottom was a cherry-red tree skirt with stitched Christmas trees wrapping around it.

"These items are beautiful. Why has Alexander not used them to decorate?"

"Maybe he didn't know. Oh shoot, do you think he should have been the one to deal with this?" The judge's lips stretched as she clenched her teeth.

"I don't think he knew about them. He has a storage room in the office. I wonder why they were in the court-room."

"I wish I knew."

"Do you want any help with these? My docket is clear as ice."

"I'd love some help. Although, I don't know if we'll be using the ornaments since we decided on a natural tree theme. And I'm not sure how much Alexander should be doing. He's already getting a tree, which seems like the best way to reinjure his back." April held up the stack of cards. "What do you think of holiday bingo? We can use them with the movie and link numbers to things such as a Christmas tree, holiday sweater, stockings, and things we know are in *Home Alone*. And the winner can win something Christmas-related."

The judge squeezed April's bicep. "I love that movie!"

The joy of the holiday seemed to have doubled since opening the long-forgotten boxes, and she couldn't wait to show Alexander.

Chapter 23

Alexander

Alexander had had worse ideas in his life, but he couldn't think of them as he eased out of his car and set a hand on his back. The tree was definitely bigger than it appeared next to the stack of others. He should've gone with a fake one, but the selection was not what he wanted. A desire to impress April with a beautiful tree overcame all other thoughts, and he knew that was why he went the route he did. Plus, he had an alternative motive for his shopping trip to town. Alexander was going to Griswold up his place, as well as his father's trailer. And he hoped it would delightfully surprise the heck out of April the next time she saw the Adams' trailers at night.

Stopping by his home first, he checked his watch as he set the bags on the kitchen table. He'd planned on going back to the library, but the trip took longer than expected. In a few hours, April would be closing up the library. He had enough time to get the surprise ready; Alexander would push through the pain. He still needed to get ready for dinner at her house and drop the tree at the library before she left.

The pain in his back caused him to sit down for a few minutes, realizing he didn't have what it would take to unload the tree on his own at this point. But he couldn't cancel. He'd been looking forward to watching *A White Christmas* with April the second he thought of it.

But he couldn't leave the tree strapped to the roof of his car. It was supposed to rain again tonight. "The desert is against me, Cora." He spoke to the cat as she lapped up the water in her bowl. "When has it ever rained two days in a row?"

"Be right back." He pushed through the pain, locked up, and headed back to his car. His cell phone rang, and he glanced down to see it was April calling.

"Hi, I'm sorry it's taking me longer than expected. I have the tree, and I'm almost to the library. Are you still there?"

"Absolutely, I've been adding some finishing touches. I have something to surprise you with anyways. I was calling to see how much longer you'd be."

He started up the car. "Can you meet me out front in a few seconds?"

"Will do, bye."

As he pulled the car up to the front of the city center, the few white clouds gave way to gray clouds coming over the mountain ranges in the distance, and the lights on the cacti cast a colorful ambiance in the vacant parking lot.

Stepping out of his car, he noticed the temperature had taken a dive, and with a slight breeze, it felt nearly winter outside. The tip of his nose had a chill, but when April appeared on the curb in her evergreen-colored coat, everything in him warmed. She'd taken down her hair, and it fluttered in the wind.

"Hi." He shook the thought because she would never be with a man like him. They were spending time together because the holidays called for it, and so did his back. After all, they could be friends, nothing wrong with that. "Thanks for waiting. I'm not sure how much help I'll be. Is anyone still inside?"

"No, but I can manage the tree on my own. We don't need you hurting your back."

"It's not very gentlemanly of me to make you do something on your own."

"Good thing this isn't 1952, then." She winked and undid the string from the tree. "It's full but shorter than the one I set on fire, and I managed to drag that bad boy inside all by myself."

"You know, there's a cart in the office. I haven't used it in years, since I haven't had to move a massive amount of books, but if you can get the tree on there, then it can easily be pushed in."

"What a great idea. I'll grab it. Wait here, I don't want to ruin your surprise." She hurried off, and her loose curls bounced against her neck.

He shivered as the breeze chilled him even more, and his ears tingled. It had to have been at least fifty degrees. Blustery for sure, but it would make watching a movie and enjoying a beverage the perfect evening. Yet, the mention of a surprise caused him to lean and try to see through the main doors into the library. However, the distance was too grand to make out anything. Racking his brain, he couldn't think of what the surprise might be.

Alexander removed the remaining two shopping bags from the floorboard of this car. The bags held multicolored Christmas lights in mini and standard sizes, red and white throw pillows for the chairs, and window clings of delightful poinsettias and warm holiday greetings.

The sound of squeaky wheels grew louder as April returned with the dolly cart. "Can you help me support it as I get it set on here?"

He nodded, and with her doing most of the work, they got the tree upright onto the cart, and she spun around and walked backward, taking the cart with her.

Alexander left his car unlocked with his bags in hand and followed her inside. It was when the tree passed over the library door's threshold that he saw the surprise April had mentioned.

She pulled the tree off to the side and allowed him to step past her and take in the view. His eyes didn't know where to start. On the ceiling were strings of white lights and hanging lower were intricately cut paper snowflakes. Even though the Christmas tree was not yet in place, the library showcased delicate beauty. Something tugged at his heart as he stepped farther inside. The myriad of snowflakes caused a rush of memories, and he didn't see how anyone could make that amount fast enough, plus hang them.

"These snowflakes . . ." He stood under them to examine them better. "They look familiar."

"They should. The judge found two boxes . . . from the time your mom was here."

His breath escaped him. "Goodness, yes." His eyes stayed glued to the snowflakes. He'd made some of them with his mom. "I can't believe this is all still here. I never knew. I figured they'd been thrown out when she retired since I'd never seen them in the office."

"I'm glad to see you're happy about this. I wasn't sure if, well, if it would be hard to see this stuff. I guess everyone reacts differently to memories."

He continued studying them. "It's comforting and angelic. A memory I thought was lost, and you found it."

"Technically, the judge did. And there are boxes of ornaments for the tree, but I know we wanted to go natural this year. The extra lights came from the box, but they're old, so we'll have to make sure we turn them off when we leave since they aren't LED."

"Do you mind if we finish everything tomorrow morning?" he asked.

She paused and tilted her head. "Sure. I'm actually pretty tired."

He looked down at his shoes. "Right, it's been a long day for us both."

"You're still coming over, right?"

He looked at April and half-smiled. "Yes, as long as I can sit down."

"All you need to do is show up with the movie." April grabbed her purse and Frank's leash and gave him a quick wave as she hurried to the main doors.

And as he locked up, all he could think about was wanting to watch every movie ever made if it meant spending time with April.

Chapter 24

April

"We're going to need a do-over." She cleared the plates from the coffee table and set them in the sink.

"What do you mean?" Alexander lifted his arm off Frank's back. The two had become quick buddies in the last two hours while the bulldog snuggled up against Alexander as though he were a warm blanket on a cold night.

"That was not a Christmas movie. Classic movie, okay, I can give you that, but nothing about it was Christmassy. It lacked decorations and even Christmas colors."

"The beginning and the end had some garland and a Christmas tree or two."

"Tell me the real reason you watch it every year."

"My mom," Alexander said, "it was one of the ones she watched every year. She loved Christmas and watching her favorite movies with her created memories I cherish today. However, my dad hated *A White Christmas*. Thus, he would agree with you."

April's eyes locked on Alexander with the intensity of someone trying to memorize his appearance. She knew it was because she'd missed him when she left, and something tugged at her to mention the job interview, but there was already enough on both of their plates with the library celebration and Christmas right around the corner. Tomorrow would be the final touches in the library and then a busy morning of setting up the activities following that.

"I bet you don't own a true classic movie," he stated. "Christmas or not."

"I do. But what do you consider classic? Does it have to be black-and-white?"

"Anything beyond the last, let's go with, thirty-five years. There are only so many Christmas movies made, even fewer worth watching."

"Then I definitely have a classic Christmas movie." She leaned over the back of the couch, near his right shoulder. "Can I get you a refill on your hot chocolate?"

"No, thank you. However, I am curious about this classic movie you have in mind." He reached for his back. "I should be getting home. We have a busy day ahead of us, and my back is just about at its limit for today, and maybe then some."

April's heart sank as she hurried around the couch and lowered herself next to him just as he was standing up. Frank let out a groan of disapproval as he dipped into the couch where the cushions met. "Why didn't you say something?"

"There is nothing to be done. It needs time and rest."

She wanted to place her hand on his arm but stopped herself. Growing more attached to him by the day and connecting with him would only make things worse come the new year. "Why don't you take tomorrow off from the library? I can handle everything."

"You've already worked longer than agreed upon."

"And it's been nice." She leaned in, drawn to the scent he was wearing or maybe he simply smelled *that* good. "Don't you think?"

"Yes, it has been nice." His eyes wandered before going to her lips and then back at her eyes.

Alexander's cell phone rang in his pocket, and he pulled it out. "It's my dad." He ignored the call and put it on silent. "I should go, he might need something."

"We're still on for another Christmas movie classic, right?" She bit her lip, trying to keep from thinking about kissing him.

"Yes, how about the day after the library celebration?"

"Perfect," she sighed.

"I can't wait," he breathed, and stood.

All April could do was nod and stare at his lips, admiring the way his top lip had a slight dip in the middle. Alexander's five-o'clock shadow had started to show, and even though she knew it would tickle, she wanted to run her fingers along his chin and pull him in for a kiss.

"Sorry, again about your back. I wish you'd said something."

He stopped and turned around. "To be honest, I don't remember it hurting during the movie." Alexander reached for her right hand and brought it to his lips. Then released it and smiled.

She blushed at him kissing her hand as though they were in England. "A good movie will do that, even if it's not a Christmas movie."

He gently nodded and gave her a half-smile as he made his way to the back slider and opened it. "Good night, April."

"Good night, Alexander." She leaned on the frame for support.

He paused, his back towards her, then he eased around to face her again. "Good night, Frank," he raised his voice. "He's an interesting dog, but I mean that in a good way."

She pressed her palm against the glass, shutting it closed, and when she went to lock it, there was a soft knock on the other side. April eased it back open. "Is everything okay?"

"You can see it, right?"

April frowned. "See—" He stepped aside, and she noticed it. "Oh my!" April grabbed hold of his shoulders, and she moved past him and farther out onto the patio. "Is that your place?"

"And my dad's." A smile eased between his lips, like the joy of a child on Christmas morning opening a gift.

She stood equal to his side and kept looking at the lights. "Did you pull a Griswold? Alexander Adams, this is very uncharacteristic of you."

"Call me Alex." His smile widened.

"Alex?"

He nodded. "Yes."

April stared at him so long that she lost track of time and couldn't think of how she wanted to respond.

When he took her hand into his, she blinked and refocused. Just over his shoulder, she made out the slight display of colors strung over the cactus on the hill. Everything produced such a perfect moment that she didn't want it to end. The way his hand felt against hers, warm and comforting. The desire to turn to him and hope he kissed her sang in her veins, imploring her to do so.

She glanced down at her hand in his as he squeezed it. But she did not turn to him, and he let go, allowing it to fall back to her side. A sigh of disappointment left her lungs.

"Good night, April."

"Good night, Alex." April watched him walk across the yard back to the wash. And the sheer notion that they'd be partaking in Christmas activities together warmed her more than any amount of hot chocolate she could drink.

Chapter 25

Alex

Alex's dad rang his phone again, and again, yet he didn't answer it. He swore his racing heart caused his upper body to tremble. Had he messed up by not kissing April on the lips, or had he made the right choice to walk away? Reaching for her hand took him by surprise, as though he didn't have any other option than to follow through with what his gut instructed him to do.

As Alex reached the property, he walked the short distance to his dad's front door, guided by the Griswold lighting. Before his fist could fall upon the door, it swung open with a burst of wind.

"You didn't answer."

"My apologies, I was with April. It would've been rude to answer, interrupting our time unless there was an emergency. Plus, I was on my way over. Is everything okay?"

"Elizabeth is here." His dad said through clenched teeth. "She's trying to help me."

Alex turned around and only spotted his dad's car. "Did she walk over?"

"Come inside." William took Alex by the forearm. "And the lights look great, son. Bright enough that I can see much better outside. Thank you for finally partaking in the holiday season."

"Alexander, hi," Elizabeth said from the kitchen. "How are you?"

He stepped further into the trailer as William closed the door behind him. "I'm well. Is everything alright here?"

Elizabeth's eyes grew wide, and she used them to motion to the ham sitting in the dish.

"Dad, why don't you go and rest, watch some television? I'll help Elizabeth." Alex started toward the kitchen, but William grabbed his bicep.

"Get her to leave," his dad whispered.

Alex nodded his head. "Go watch television, Dad."

William huffed and shuffled over to his recliner as Alex approached Elizabeth.

"I had to wash the ham," she whispered.

"Wash it?" He placed his hands on his hips, observing the spiral of meat in the dish.

"It smelled like a red dirt road." She peeked around Alex. "I don't know what he thought he was seasonin' it with, but you must have a talk to him about his vision. Maybe he needs glasses or cataract surgery."

Alex rubbed at his chin and stared at the clean ham. "It's his cataracts. He refused to do any surgery, and glasses won't help."

"Then he needs to relinquish feedin' us at the Library's Christmas Celebration."

"He's been doing it since my mom was the librarian. We can't take it away from him."

"Then, he needs help. We can't allow him to serve any food without us checkin' to make sure he's not confusin' spices. I mean, doesn't he smell the difference?"

Alex cleared his throat and shoved his hands into his pockets. "He had a terrible sinus infection about ten years ago. The doctor prescribed a nasal spray to help clear it up, and he unknowingly was allergic to it." He eyed his father as he pointed the remote at the television. "He lost his sense of smell."

"He's a real package, ain't he?" Elizabeth laughed.

"My mom thought so." William crossed his arms.

The judge's hands rested on the ham, so she leaned her shoulder into Alex. "Sorry. I don't mean to be nasty."

"You didn't reside here when she was alive; it's not something you were privy to." Alex reviewed the spice containers on the counter. "I might have an idea that'll work."

The judge moved to the sink and washed her hands. "Can I be of any help?"

"We need masking tape."

"Let me go check my 1980s drawer." She dried her hands on the dish towel hanging on the oven door.

Although he understood the joke, Alex didn't laugh. Ever since he left April on the patio, all he could think about was what it might've been like to kiss her—remembering how his hand felt in hers, inviting and comfortable.

"Alexander?"

"I have masking tape." Alex removed his house keys from his pocket. "We can relabel the spices with bigger print. Hopefully, that'll stop any more confusion."

"I never thought of that. Alexander, you have so much more to offer this town with the library." Elizabeth leaned against the edge of the counter. "Yet . . ."

Alex crossed his arms over his chest. He didn't know if he wanted to hear what else the judge had to offer. However, spending time with April caused his regular notions to twist ever slightly. And a small part of him wanted to make changes. Not big ones, but the happiness he'd not felt in some time stirred inside of him.

"Please finish your sentence, Elizabeth."

The judge brought her hands to her shoulders by her neck and looked up at the ceiling. "The town wants you out. They want April to take over for you, for good."

"I didn't hear what else you two were whispering about, but I sure as tootin' hear that." William shuffled to the entrance of the kitchen.

"Dad—" Alex started.

"No, son, Elizabeth is correct." William held up his hand. "You must make changes. Your mom would've wanted things around the library to evolve."

"I know she did, Dad, but not to the extent that the town is leaning towards."

"You're wrong, and April will take your job if you don't make changes."

Alex pinched his eyes closed for two seconds, and when he opened them, he walked to the door and exited his dad's house only to be faced with the bright reminder that he'd done a lot to change already, and clearly, it wasn't enough.

Chapter 26

April

April woke with a rush of nervous excitement, and Frank's adorable blubbery cheeks hovering over her.

"I don't know what I'm more ready for, the interview or the celebration." She remained under the bed covers and folded the sheet over the comforter as she clasped her hands together on top. "Both could go wrong, but you know what, Frank, that's okay." The bulldog waddled over the top of April's legs and down the ramp onto the floor.

Through her therapy for her anxiety, April knew she needed to focus on what she could control and not what she couldn't. And then there was Alex. He simply deranged all of the plans she had and managed to braid her heart with confusion as he showed a side of himself she'd never known. Maybe he hadn't even known it was there.

As she readied herself for work, she made a careful effort to focus on her makeup. She usually stuck with a neutral palette for her day-to-day, but since it would be a video interview, she wanted to make sure she didn't appear too washed out on the laptop's camera. Plus, she wanted to put on an extra sparkle of holiday joy for the Library's Christmas Celebration.

Switching out her mauve lipstick for red and her normal terracotta-and-sand eye shadow for eggplant and royal blue, she then swapped her usual low ponytail for a chic high ponytail. Luckily, she had all her boxes of clothes from college and was able to locate her red cardigan to throw over her white blouse and paired it with jeans and black flats. Of course, Alex would object once she saw the jeans, but she would stand her ground since they would be working in the snow and with sticky candy.

Because of her black flats, she decided to drive to the library to keep as much dust off them as possible—not that the interviewer would ask April to pan down and show her shoes, but secretly she hoped someone would want to take pictures at the celebration. And with Frank, she knew all too well how often shoes ended up at the forefront of photos with dogs.

Her purse weighed heavy on her shoulder with the laptop tucked inside as she entered the library with Frank in tow and found Alex sitting at the desk.

"Good morning, April. I'm glad you're here. We have a great deal to accomplish before the celebration." Alex stood from his chair but paused midway and blinked. "You . . ."

April touched her face. "I did my makeup differently today. Does it look okay?"

Alex nodded. "Yes." He stepped forward as though to get a closer look. "It looks fine. I'm used to how you normally look. Not that you look *unnormal*." He waved his hand in her direction. "Not that you don't look great now or then."

"I'm just spiffier now."

A smile flickered across his lips. "Yes, I would agree."

"I thought all we had to do was set everything up?" April removed her jacket and hung it on the rack just inside the office door.

Frank made his way to Alex and sat at his feet. Alex reached down to give the bulldog long strokes down his back. "How've you been, Frank?"

Alex had warmed up to the dog, and April had seen an increase in him talking to Frank—something she once thought would never happen, although he did have Cora. She'd just always assumed he wasn't the type to speak to animals; that kept them as silent company.

April hung her purse with her jacket as Alex stood back up. She wasn't going to mention the interview to him, at least not until there was something to tell. Not only did it erase the pressure if she didn't land the position, but she didn't want anything to overshadow the celebration today. And after the way Alex had held her hand and left all the emotions hanging, she couldn't stand any more complications.

Alex gazed at the Christmas tree in the middle of the room. April couldn't allow her thoughts to wander to Alex during the interview. She had to focus.

"Was everything okay with your dad last night?"

Alex turned to her. "Yes, the judge was over. His vision issues had created problems with the ham for today. However, we remedied the cooking situation."

Before April could answer, the sound of shoes moving quickly into the room caused them to turn and face the library door.

"Alexander, good morning. And April, to you as well." Charlie Tow approached the desk wearing his traditional floral button-down short-sleeve shirt, cargo shorts, and panic across his face. "And Frank! I almost didn't see you there." Charlie gave a low and short wave at the bulldog. "Alexander, if we might have a word?"

"April knows, Charlie." Alex moved his hands to his pockets.

"She knows?" Charlie's eyebrows flexed.

Anyone in town would tell you that Charlie could relay every expression available without a word and just the movement of his eyebrows.

"I saw you leaving the library late one night, and—" April paused, not wanting to spoil the surprise of who the mystery lady was.

"I'm afraid I allowed it to slip out," Alex interjected.

"I'm sorry if I wasn't to know, but I've not mentioned it to anyone." April glanced at Alex and then back at Charlie.

"It's okay, after all, I suppose, since today I'm meeting Desert Girl in person."

April tapped her foot. "Finally, it's about time. I hear this online chatting has been going on for some time."

"We both needed to be ready. However, our date is rather unorthodox if I do say so." Charlie removed his cell from his pocket and checked it. "We're meeting at the celebration today, and then if all goes well, knowing who we are, we're going to take a hike up the hill to see what clues might be on the lighted cacti as to who did it this year. I wanted to make sure she feels safe. You just never know these days. And since she knew about the cacti, she's a local. I just can't for the life of my figure out who Desert Gal is."

"Well then, I guess I can check off you and your mystery lady as being the decorator for this year's cacti." April winked.

"I'm still unsure how you both have gone this long and not exchanged a photo or even your real names." Alex grabbed his coffee mug off the desk and took a drink. "I've been curious as to who it could be. There are not a lot of single women in town."

April pressed her hands together at a point near her chin.

"It's not you, right?" Charlie's eyebrows wiggled.

"Sorry, Charlie." April smiled.

Charlie clapped his hands together. "The reason for my visit this morning is we both wanted to meet someplace a little quieter during the celebration and wondered if maybe we could do so here before the movie when everyone is out doing the other activities."

"That will be so magical." April pointed. "We'll turn on the string lights, and with the glow of the Christmas tree, oh, it'll be like a romantic movie from the nineties."

Charlie reached his hand out to April's shoulder. "Thank you. Let's hope it has a delightful nineties ending."

She watched as Charlie left the library, and when she turned to Alex, she caught him staring at her, and instantly her cheeks warmed. "What?"

"I'm glad you're here . . . to help with the celebration . . . and allowing me to realize change can be a good thing."

"I'm surprised you're alright with making changes."

"With your help, of course. I mean, before you leave. I understand you won't be staying."

Her joy faded like a dusting of pollen in the air. "Correct, I won't be staying." Regardless, hearing him say it meant he'd accepted that nothing could ever happen between them. "And I'm happy to help."

"Thank you."

She wanted to ask him about last night. About why they didn't kiss her on the lips. "How's your back?"

"It's doing as well as I can expect." Alex gazed around the room. "I've appreciated all your assistance with the library and wanted to pick your brain, if I may, about implementing several of your ideas."

"Right now?" April pointed at the ground.

"If you have time, possibly tomorrow? Unless you have other plans?"

"But the library is closed tomorrow due to the celebration today."

"Yes, and I thought we were going to watch the surprise classic movie together?"

"Yes, we are." April smiled at the thought. "And I'd be more than happy to go over anything you wish. But right now, we have a celebration to get set up for."

As April pulled out her notepad with the checklist, she used it to fan her face. The thought of spending time alone again with Alex made her exuberant.

Chapter 27

Alex

Charlie entered the city center wearing the same thing he wore this morning. Alex gave him a nod and watched him head into the empty library. April had turned on the Christmas lights, and the room glowed with a cozy ambience.

Outside the library doors, however, was a different story. Folding tables covered in Christmas-themed plastic tablecloths lined the middle of the hall. Families gathered around, working on constructing their graham cracker gingerbread houses.

Festive, traditional Christmas music filtered through the CD player that sat on the table with the refreshments. April observed the gingerbread table when she spotted Charlie going into the library and hurried to Alex.

"So, have you seen any women head into the library yet?" she asked, standing on Alex's left.

He shook his head. "I can't imagine how nervous he must be."

"I can't believe you know who the woman is, and I don't. I know she's local but—" he paused when Lillian eased her way through the main doors.

Alex felt April's hand find his arm and her fingers wrapping around, squeezing slightly.

"Lillian? How could I not have put it together?" He observed Lillian cross the middle of the hall.

"They're about the same age. I wasn't sure about her and R. J.—I thought they might finally get together—but once the judge and R. J. made their relationship known, I guess it was easier to put it together, plus I had the upper hand after I spoke with Lillian."

"I feel left out for some reason." Alex turned to her.

"Don't. R. J. and Lillian got together a great deal when I worked at Luis's restaurant, and now that I think about it, Charlie did come into the diner and sit at the bar so he could chat with her through the kitchen window." She took Alex's hand. "Come on, let's go watch."

Alex wiggled his feet in his shoes. "We can't do that."

"You believe in love, don't you?"

He faced April. "Yes, but I don't see what that has to do with spying on them."

"It's either that or you get messy with the gingerbread house making."

"Alright." Alex allowed April to guide him by the hand to the library's door right behind Lillian entering through it.

Charlie had his back turned to the door and didn't see her stepping closer. He was standing at the Christmas tree, most likely admiring the vintage ornaments they'd agreed to put on in the final minutes. Lillian paused in her steps, obviously aware of who the mystery man was, and Alex noticed her head lean a few inches to the side as though her body relaxed, spotting Charlie.

April pressed into Alex as she felt his breath on her neck and his hand over her shoulder. "Oh goodness, I feel like we're watching a movie," she whispered.

Lillian took two more steps forward, and then just as she was about to tap Charlie on the shoulder, he swiveled around.

"Lil?" Charlie questioned, seeming as though in disbelief as his eyebrows dipped.

"Hi, Charlie. Or should I call you Desert Guy?"

Alex attempted to turn around. "We shouldn't be interfering." But April was pressed against him so that he couldn't move.

"Shh, we're just making sure this is safe. You never know who you'll meet on the Internet these days."

"But we did know, and now they know," Alex whispered.

"Shh, this stuff never happens in real life. Let me enjoy it for a few more seconds."

"Of course love like this happens. People often don't see what's right in front of them." And he'd never spoken truer words.

"Do you need any assistance?" April leaned in his direction.

Alex was at the end of the table, attempting to build a gingerbread house. And there couldn't have been a better example of the word *attempt* than him right at that moment.

"It's okay if you roll up your sleeves. Literally. Roll them up." April placed green and red gummy candies onto the roof of her gingerbread.

He glanced at the wrists of his button-down shirt and then at his hands, both covered in a sticky frosting mess.

"Here"—April wiped her hands on a wet wipe—"let me roll them up for you."

Her fingers brushed against the skin on his wrist, and he swallowed hard, trying to keep his thoughts from traveling to where they shouldn't. Holding his other arm out, April rolled up the sleeve to his elbow.

"There you go." She patted his arm. "Now, get back to work. We have snow coming in less than half an hour."

He returned to his gingerbread, but it looked like more of a hut than a house. The entire thing leaned to the right and had massive amounts of frosting at the base but barely any at the seams. Alex glanced over at April's and noticed how perfect her house appeared, as though she practiced making them weekly. The notion of her leaving soon caused his hands to fumble with the wafer cookies before they reached the pathway to the house. If only there were a way they could both work at the library so she could stay. However, no matter what direction he thought, Alex kept coming up empty. He'd have to make the best of the time they had together, and when it was over, it would be what it had to be.

April nudged Alex with her elbow and motioned for him to look up. When he did, Lillian and Charlie were, at last, exiting the library. He didn't know how much time had passed since they'd been there, but long enough to have an extended chat.

Lillian had looped her hand around the crook of Charlie's arm and her head laid on his shoulder as they walked past the gingerbread table as though they were the only two around.

Charlie pushed the main door open, and they stepped outside without Lillian lifting her head from the spot.

"They're so in love. I think they fell in love a long time ago." April placed a peppermint into her mouth.

"You believe they could've?"

April nodded and kept staring in the direction of the main doors. "Yes, just because they hadn't realized who was who until now, or because it was online, doesn't mean anything."

"Do you think people can be in love who aren't to-gether? I mean, such as a long-distance relationship?"

"I believe it can be possible. But I also think it depends on the person and the relationship goals." April checked her cell phone, then slid it back into her pocket.

"Do you have goals for a relationship?"

"Of course I do. What about you?" She popped a few white chocolate chips into her mouth.

"I never thought I would. However, things change." He smiled and glanced at his gingerbread house. "Things can change for the better, even if one never recognizes the need until it's right in front of them."

Chapter 28

April

The snow made the cool air even chillier, but April loved to watch the kids form snowballs and make snow angels. Frank was hanging out with Trinity and Jolie, the little girl leading him around in the snow by his leash. It had been a good day so far, and she couldn't recall the last time she'd seen so many smiles at once—Alex among them.

She removed her cell from her pocket again; it was nearly time to get her laptop ready for the interview. Looking around, she spotted Alex coming across the way. He'd stayed behind to wrap up the last families working on their gingerbread houses.

"I'm really impressed with this year's celebration—the best ever," Wyatt Hackenberg said as he took a shot from the snowball thrown by his daughter, Jasmine. "We do hope you can stay and show Alexander your ways."

"Don't worry, Alex will come around to change, but I won't be staying." April rubbed the sides of her arms as the frigid air was getting to her without a jacket on.

Dressed in a pea coat, Alex carefully bent down to a pile of snow. April focused on his movements and wondered what was happening.

Is Alex playing in the snow?

Then, *smack*, a freezing snowball hit her arm. Her mouth formed an O. *Did that just happen?*

"Alex!" She squatted and gathered a clump of snow forming in between her palms. When April stood up, another snowball smacked her left knee.

Alex chuckled and dashed to the right of the snow pile as April hurtled a snowball in his direction. It made contact with the back of his shoulder. She had to be careful not to hit his lower back.

He pivoted around, and when they made eye contact, it was as though there was not another soul in sight. Alex's smile radiated bright enough to melt the snow.

"I'm surprised by you." April kneeled, forming another snowball.

"Then I'm grateful to surprise you." And without seeing where he had stored it, a snowball flew at her, smacking between her ear and shoulder.

April shrieked and ran after Alex, who spun around but had nowhere to go with the school's wall on one side and a set of swings on the other. She met him with her hands outstretched, landing on his shoulders.

She caught her breath, not from the activity but from the excitement and endorphins. Alex's hands found her waist. The firmness of his palms pressing into her sides kept her feeling stable at the edge of the snowbank.

"Is your back okay?" Her hand wrapped around his bicep.

"I completely forgot."

She tilted her head and let her hand fall to her side. "You forgot you had a back?"

He nodded. "Your eyes have compassion and sincerity in their sparkle."

Feeling the warmth grow in her cheeks, she looked over his shoulder, trying to remedy it.

"April?" Alex's voice was smooth like caramel swirled atop hot coffee.

"Mm-hmm?" *Oh no, don't look at him. Don't!*

His hand moved to her chin, tilted her head, and they locked eyes. When her vision paired with Alex's, she noticed his rain cloud gray eyes were like looking at the perfect storm. She was like snow in the sun and melted into him, wrapping her arms around his neck as his hand found her waist again.

Are we swaying in slow motion? Is music playing?

The alarm on her cell phone in her pocket went off. She licked her lips as Alex pulled back, his hands letting go of her waist.

"Sorry about that." April removed her phone and ended the alarm sound. "Crap. I've got to head inside. I have something I must do."

Alex stepped back and turned around, defeat plastered across his face. "Good idea, you look cold. I can manage for now."

"Thank you." She pressed her lips together and made her way back across the parking lot and down the short path back to the city center.

Once inside, she took her laptop out, set it on the office desk, and closed the door. With everyone out playing in the snow, she had a little bit of time before William showed up with the food, and they would be starting the movie.

Although April could have sworn she'd already done so a second ago, she punched the power button again. Yet the laptop remained silent, and the keyboard didn't backlight itself. April's eyebrows creased between the bridge of her nose.

"No, no, no," she hissed.

April shook the laptop in front of her. When she set it back down, she pressed her pointer finger into the power button hard and long enough for the tip of her finger to turn white.

"Why is this happening to me?" April raised her finger and then returned it, tapping the power button repeatedly.

Checking her cell phone for the time, she clenched her teeth, drew her hands to her face, and let out a shriek that matched a frazzled cartoon character.

"Think!" April didn't have to look far to see the computer monitor next to her broken laptop.

A gentle knock tapped the door. "April?"

She blinked and eased open the office door. "Alex?"

He stepped closer, his hand moving to the doorknob as she stepped back, closer to the desk.

"What are you doing?" Alex glanced at the computer and then moved to see the front of her dark laptop screen.

Her mouth opened, but all that came out was a sigh. "Alex"—she scratched at the back of her hair—"I thought you were managing the snow play?"

"I needed you." He stepped forward, appearing out of breath as though he'd run to the library.

"I have an interview."

Alex paused, and his hand fell from the door's knob. Watching him blink as though confusion tore at his heart.

Of course she had an interview; she *needed* to have an interview. However, that wasn't what caused her trepidation. It was what the interview meant. It meant she'd be leaving, and anything that might, or could, romantically happen between them never would.

Chapter 29

Alex

"Alex?" William's voice traveled from the main hall, finding Alex rushing out the library's door. "Alex?"

He'd gone to find April because he had to kiss her. He needed to. Yet when she mentioned the interview, he felt like he'd been stabbed. She'd changed him in many ways, and the most obvious was in his dramatic thoughts. April had penetrated his heart. He busied himself with cleaning up the gingerbread house tables, and after a bit of time, the tables were ready for his dad's ham, the side dishes, and pizza for the kids.

"Dad? Why are you carrying the ham? You can barely see over it." Alex reached for the tray as it started to slip from William's grip.

"Because I was on the run from Elizabeth."

"Can you even see that far?" Alex set the warm, golden ham at the end of the table.

"I felt the wind shift."

Alex huffed and crossed his arms. "That's harsh."

"You ask Trinity and Camden if they think so, then we'll talk." William glanced around. "Am I early?"

"Right on time, Dad." Alex checked his wristwatch. "I put the pizza order in with Luis a few minutes ago." He glanced back at the library door. April was still in the office, and the interview took longer than Alex thought it might.

"Where's April?" William asked.

"She's . . . she's in the office." Alex scratched at his left eyebrow. "She's in the middle of an interview. Or maybe the end of an interview."

"And how do you feel about that, son?"

Alex took a deep breath, allowing his eyes to close with the inhale. And when he released it, his eyes opened. "There is no way to feel about it. I'm the librarian in this town, and there isn't room for the two of us. She deserves to land a position at a place that is as grand as she is."

William removed his hat and fiddled with the closure on the back. "I suppose you're right."

"How do you think the ham turned out?"

William glanced at the spiral. "I believe it came out well, thanks to you. I have to turn all my spice bottles nearly 360 degrees to read all the words, but at least I can read them now."

The city center's door opened behind them, and they turned around. The judge entered carrying a Corning-Ware casserole dish with tin foil draped over the top.

"Who's ready to dig into my Blend of the Bayou?" Elizabeth raised the dish slightly and gave it a wiggle.

"That sounds . . . I'm not sure," William laughed.

"William, you'll love it. It's got cream cheese, mushrooms, and shrimp." The judge set the dish next to the platter of ham.

"Hard to go wrong with that combination." William licked his top lip.

"Gavin should be comin' along with Aurora and her girls. They made biscuits." Elizabeth rubbed her hands together. "This year's library celebration has been smashin'. I'm glad the kids are gettin' pizza, more food for us adults."

"Speak for yourself, Judge. I'm having a slice of pizza, too." William patted his stomach. "I hope we have extra-large paper plates."

Alex shook his head with a chuckle. He enjoyed being able to count on things in life and familiarities. And his father's appetite was one of them.

"I assume R. J. is coming once he closes up his store for the day?" Alex asked.

Elizabeth nodded. "Yes, he's bringin' the drinks."

"Great, thank you. I'd better get the movie set up for the kids." Alex entered the library as April emerged from the office.

They froze in their respective spots.

"I'm sorry, Alex. I should've told you sooner." April stepped forward and closed the office door behind her. "We know I can't stay."

"You're correct."

"I'm not sure exactly why I felt the need to hide it from you. I suppose because I've enjoyed our time together.

And . . ." April waved her hand in the air in a *never mind* movement. "It doesn't matter."

Alex stepped closer, the library around him blurring. "It does matter. What were you going to say?"

April brought her hands together and lowered her head, appearing to focus on her flats.

"There you two are," Luis stated, carrying pizza boxes into the library. "I didn't know if there was enough room on the tables for all these." He halted and looked around. "Wow, this place looks amazing."

"It's all thanks to April." Alex motioned with his hand as he went to Luis, taking half the boxes. "I can't believe I'm going to say this. Let's set these over on the table in the kid's reading section."

"Well, April, bravo." Luis followed Alex with the remaining pizzas. "I made sure to have Lillian prep two cheese-only pizzas, one pepperoni, one with sauce only—as I know Ralph is coming—and two for the adults, just in case the ham didn't turn out." He opened the lids on two boxes. "Sausage and olives, bacon and pineapple."

"A kid might want those toppings; you never know." April peeked at the boxes.

"I believe I'll steal one of the children's cheese pizza slices." Alex moved the small chairs out of the way from under the table. "I'm not big on ham, but I'm intrigued by what the judge brought, some blended swamp thing."

April stepped next to Alex and helped him stack the chairs out of the way. "Bayou, Blended Bayou."

"Where is your dog, April?" Luis peeked around the front desk.

"He's with Trinity and Jolie. I think he's having more fun with them than me."

"I'll set aside a little bit of William's ham for you to surprise him with." Luis squeezed April's shoulder.

Lillian entered through the library doors, without her new boyfriend.

"And where is Charlie?" April inquired, tilting her head. "Did your hike up the mountain to the cacti lead to anything?"

"We never made it." Lillian's cheeks turned the color of blooming pink roses. "He'll be here shortly, but"—she looked over April's shoulder—"we're unlikely to stay long. We plan to make the cacti inquiry during our moonlit walk."

"That sounds lovely," April beamed.

Lillian glanced over at Alex, then back at April. He noticed but pretended he didn't, looking down at the carpet.

"You two," Lillian said and shook her head as she headed out of the library along with Luis.

Alex was acutely aware that he was once again alone with April. His heart thumped in his chest, and his vision traveled around, hoping for a child to come running in.

"Alex, I—" April started.

He flipped up the lid on one of the boxes and grabbed a slice of pizza, shoving it into his mouth.

"Alex?"

Putting his hand over his mouth, he mumbled, "Better finish setting up."

The last thing he wanted to do was follow through on his feelings. And he didn't need to know what April tried to tell him. It would undoubtedly make him question everything or break his heart.

As children began entering the library, Alex felt a sense of relief that the pizza hadn't been able to accomplish. He waved them over to the table, and after grabbing their pizza, he instructed them to find a spot in front of the makeshift screen.

"Alexander, this is amazing," Trinity said as she looked around, allowing April to take back Frank's leash. "And look at you—allowing children to eat and drink around these books."

"All for the better." Trinity helped her daughter put a slice onto the paper plate.

Alex snuck a peek at April, who had lowered to Frank to indulge him in an overall body rub.

A smile creased his lips. "I do assume it's all for the best. No point in being a scrooge for another Christmas."

Trinity caught hold of Alex peering at April and let him know he'd been caught by giving him a wink. He watched as more children entered the library, then he showed them where to get their plates and drinks.

A hand touched his shoulder, and when he turned around, April was there. "I wanted to say I look forward to our movie night. As long as it's still on."

Her eyes held hope, and he couldn't help but sneak a look at her lips. He'd longed to kiss them, regardless of her leaving and zero chance of a relationship.

"Yes, however, I thought we should take advantage of the library's mock movie screen and view it here."

April's shoulders rose, and a grand smile formed. "That's a brilliant idea, Alex."

"Good, then I look forward to it." He gave her a quick smile before going to prepare *Home Alone*. And he meant it, even if the thought of her leaving would make not kissing her impossible.

Chapter 30

April

April wasn't sure if she'd done well or not at the interview. She'd been focused and ready, and then as soon as Alex found her in the office, with *that* look on his face, it caused her to be a stuttering mess. Thankfully, she'd been able to use his computer for the interview, but it also left a pit of regret in her stomach, as though making the secret worse.

"I should've had you with me." She snuggled up with Frank on the couch.

She was still in her interview attire, not having the energy to change into her pajamas. But truthfully, April wouldn't be surprised if she woke in the morning with dog hair in her mouth and lipstick on the couch pillow.

She sat up far enough to reach for her glass of Moscato. The bowl of popcorn was nestled between her and the pillow, and she grabbed a handful, shoving it into her mouth. When she closed her eyes, April thought about the beauty of the Washington State Law Library she'd interviewed with. A true dream job.

It was an effort to push past her sadness about having to leave Woolsey in her rearview mirror. Then April's thoughts turned to the *Woolsey Times* and how she'd yet again have to turn over the reins to Jennifer. A part of her would miss the fun it brought to do something meaningful for the town.

She sipped the Moscato and wrapped her hand around the stem. "I can't stay. There is no room for me here. No future."

Yet, maybe it wasn't only about Alex. Maybe it was about Woolsey. Maybe it was about both. She'd been so happy with her return home. Waking up to the desert sunrises. Enjoying the cool temperatures in the morning and the warm sunshine in the afternoons was something she couldn't get in Washington. Then there was the joy of knowing everyone and not having to be worried about things being crowded, even if people gathered. Yesterday, in spite of all the residents being in attendance, the numbers were a far cry from even one of her large classes at the university or the cafeteria on campus.

The head of the interview committee did confirm that Frank would be welcome if she was offered the position, which was a requirement at any job she landed outside of a small town. April turned her vision to the Christmas tree in the corner of the living room. She took in the way the multicolored lights blurred between the branches and admired how the star atop shone diamond patterns on the wall behind it. The peace of the season filled her as she took a deep breath. There were so many reasons to feel blessed, yet something was missing—like a classic hardcover novel placed between mass-market paperbacks on a shelf. Sure, they were both novels, but there was something to the classic that made it fit better on the mahogany shelves.

The doorbell chimed through the house, startling both April and Frank. She wasn't expecting anyone and checked the mirror to make sure her makeup hadn't smeared before opening the front door.

"Judge?"

"Hi, sweetie, I hope you don't mind me stoppin' by," Elizabeth said and held up a small wicker basket with a tea towel covering the top.

"I'm surprised but welcome your visit." April stepped aside, allowing the judge to come in.

This wasn't the first time Elizabeth had been over for dinner, as she had dined with her parents before, but April had never spent one-on-one time with her outside of town gatherings.

"I made beignets." She set the basket on the kitchen table. "Let's say I've been bakin' for R. J. so much that I think he went up a pant size. So therefore, he appreciates me sharin' the wealth."

April laughed as she gathered two dessert plates from the cupboard. "I've never had beignets before."

"Then I'm glad I dropped by." Elizabeth removed the cloth from the basket. "And they're still warm."

They sat opposite each other at the kitchen table, the basket of power sugar-covered beignets between them. Frank, hoping for a morsel, laid at the base of April's chair.

"What do you plan to do?" The judge took a sip of the Moscato April had poured her.

"Plan?" April picked up one of the beignets and brought it to her lips.

"Yes, about being in love with Alexander?"

April coughed and powder sugar dispersed in a puff in front of her. "In love?"

"Why yes. The entire town sees it."

"Sees it?"

"It's already past my bedtime, April, let's not dance around it. Alexander is happier than a dead pig in the sunshine."

"That's an odd reference." April allowed the dough to melt on her tongue. "But do you think?"

"Of course, hon. He's in love with you."

Hearing the words caused the vision of those mass-market paperbacks to fall off the imaginary shelf. Alex was the classic hardcover novel, and she was a paperback. "I had an interview today for a librarian spot at the Washington State Law Library in Olympia."

"Well, why did you do that?" Elizabeth tucked one of her wildly curly chili-colored hair strands behind her ear.

"Because the library is Alexander's. It's not my job to take." April bit her lower lip. "Besides, he's going to make the changes around there. It will be wonderful. Just wait and see."

"Oh, I'm not worried about the changes. I'm worried about you two allowin' the perfect relationship to slip away."

April swallowed a sip of wine, and it felt hard, like a rock in her throat. "Perfect? Did I miss something?"

"You're old enough to understand opposites attract."

April picked up another piece of beignet. "Yes, but I'm not staying in town. And Alex is completely happy with his single life. The last thing he wants or needs is . . . me."

"Maybe what he needs is for you to let him know how you feel about him." The judge held her wineglass by the stem and leaned back in the chair. "Don't make me order you to do it." She winked.

"But what would telling him do?" April stared at her empty dessert plate.

Elizabeth's hand reached out and landed on April's arm. "Change everythin'."

Chapter 31

Alex

The following night, Alex double-checked his watch. April should be arriving any minute, and he loved that she understood the importance of being punctual. The library was filled with the scent of garlic bread that rested under tin foil on the nearby table. He placed the bowl of noodle-covered sauce into an insulated casserole container to keep it warm. Since he was still on pain medication, he couldn't drink any alcohol, but he didn't want to keep April from enjoying some. After all, they'd put a great deal of work into the library celebration last night, and while its success was an award in itself, wine was always a nice extra.

He had picked up some sparkling apple cider for himself and had it chilling along with a bottle of Zinfandel in two small buckets of ice he'd grabbed from the city center's break room.

Alex had the Christmas tree lights on and four large throw pillows set out on a blanket spread across the floor in front of the makeshift movie screen they'd used for *Home Alone* during the Christmas celebration.

Footsteps made their way into the library, and Alexander spun around, excited to find April.

"Good evening, Alex." She wore jeans, hunter-green heels, and an oversize knit cardigan in sage green.

"Hello, April. You look comfortable." *Comfortable? She's beautiful!* He rubbed at his forehead.

"Thanks?" April set her purse on the nearest plum chair. "I'm super excited since I haven't watched this classic in years. Any guesses?"

He slid his hands into his pockets. "No idea."

She wiggled the DVD at him, and he read aloud, "*Ernest Saves Christmas*. That's a new one on me."

"Good! Wow, it smells yummy in here. But you weren't supposed to cook."

"I didn't, Lillian did. I don't think the library has ever smelled this good before."

She giggled and covered her mouth. "I don't think a library is supposed to smell like anything other than books."

He nodded and approached her, unsure what he was going to do—hug her . . . or . . . he had no idea—until he found himself an arm's length away, and his hand found her arm. Alex squeezed her wrist as she peered down at his fingers.

What was that?!

Before turning around to hide, he picked up on the soft scent of honeydew and found it made his heart rate speed up.

"Do you want me to take over so you can sit down and rest your back?" She spotted the food on the table.

"What kind of host would I be if I allowed that?" He held up the Zinfandel and an empty wineglass.

"That would be lovely, but what about you?"

"I'm having sparkling apple."

"Well, as soon as you're off the pain meds, we'll have to get together and enjoy some wine." She took the glass as he handed it to her. Their fingertips touched again, and they held them there for longer than expected before letting go.

"I'd love that." Alex froze. *She won't be in town by then.* "Dinner is ready."

Removing the foil from the bread and taking off the lid for the spaghetti, Alex handed a plate to April.

"This is a fancy picnic. Real plates." She cupped it in both hands.

"I have any spices you might need over on the desk. I figure you won't know what it's lacking until you take a bite."

She approached Alex, and her shoulder rubbed against his. When April glanced over, her hand rested on the serving spoon sitting on the casserole container. "I'm sure I'll love it."

All he could do was nod like some idiot. Then they took their plates to the blanket, and she set hers down before walking over to the DVD player and popping the disc in.

"I'm excited to see *Ernie Saves Christmas*—a so-called classic."

He spun the spaghetti on his fork while she smiled and laughed as she sat down. Picking up her plate and resting it on her lap, she said, "Ernest. Not Ernie, although that might be a good movie if Burt agrees. Are you sure you can sit on the ground like this?"

He felt flush with her closeness. "The pillows help, plus I'm healing well."

The movie started, and classic Christmas images appeared. She leaned back before taking a chunk out of her garlic bread. "I think you might be a little put off at first but give it time. You'll enjoy it."

He'd wager he'd enjoy anything as long as they were together, even spilling spaghetti sauce on the carpet. They laughed at all the same parts, and he had such joy that he forgot about his back pain. Every stress he had was pulled from his mind as he focused on the movie. He kept staring at the sheet when the credits rolled, not wanting the evening to end.

"Do you have time for another movie? Or no, you probably have plans or . . ." he mumbled.

She shook her head, and he was mildly aware they were sharing a blanket and sitting close enough that their legs touched under it. Then, just as she opened her mouth, a ring came from inside of her purse.

"Oh shoot, it's my phone. Excuse me. It could be my parents." She set her part of the blanket aside and hurried to her phone. "Hello."

He hit end on the DVD remote and got up to clear their plates, not wanting to eavesdrop on her call. But there was no place for him to disappear to, and he noticed whoever was on the other end of the call took April by surprise because her voice was sharp in tone, and she fumbled with her words a bit.

When he returned from the break room, he found her sitting sideways on the plum chair, and when she looked up at him, he swore tears formed at the edges of her lids. "I didn't get the position in Olympia, the one I interviewed for the other day."

"That's . . ." He swallowed what felt like a paver stone. "That's, oh, no."

April stood, her focus down at the ground. She took two steps forward and lifted her head, their eyes meeting. "Yeah, *oh* is right. I don't know what I'm going to do."

"You'll figure something out." He shook his head and found his hands moving to her waist.

She mirrored him and nodded along, her arms sliding loose around his neck. Together, they started to sway without a sound in the room. April rested her cheek on his chest, and he wrapped his hands tighter around her waist, pulling her into him.

He has no idea how long they stood there, swaying to the silence. Alex knew if he let go of April, he'd have to kiss her. With her head resting on his chest, he could stay like this forever. He squeezed his arms around her, trying to keep her from retreating.

The swaying stopped, and her arms loosened around his neck. "Alex?"

"Mm-hmm." When their eyes locked, he was a goner. His right hand wrapped around the back of her head, and the other remained on her waist.

There was no resistance as Alex pulled April into a kiss. It was everything he'd thought it would be for the last several weeks and, to be honest, what he'd dreamt about in high school. He'd wanted her for far too long to keep track.

When their lips parted, their hands remained. "Well, this makes things a lot more complicated," April breathed.

He gave a quick nod and pulled her close, kissing her as though it was the first time all over again.

Chapter 32

April

April sat cross-legged on her parents' couch the following morning and balanced a cup of Christmas blend tea. The aroma of cloves, orange peel, and cinnamon steamed from the snowman mug. On the television, classic Christmas songs played softly enough that she couldn't make out all the lyrics but knew them by heart as she hummed along.

Thoughts of Alex's lips on hers caused April to wonder if not getting the job in Olympia was a sign or only a coincidence. Either way, things developing with Alex only made finding a job more difficult. She had to do it, but what would that mean if they wanted to have a relationship?

April had two more interviews lined up, one in Texas and one in Oregon. It was something she never realized but should've—finding a job as a librarian was a challenge. While every state had them, their turnover rate was nearly nonexistent.

Her cell phone rang, and she swiped it off the coffee table. Before answering, she muted the TV and noticed the call was coming from a Washington area code.

"Hello?" April quickly sipped her tea to coat her suddenly dry throat.

"Ms. Gardner, this is Miranda at the Washington State Law Library."

"Yes, hello, how can I be of help?"

"I admit it's uncomfortable to call someone we turned down for a position."

April rolled her eyes and took another sip from the mug. "But Ms. Gardner, you and your dog Frank . . . See, I've been in contact with Jack Randall, and I recommended you for a position he's trying to fill."

Frank repositioned himself on the couch next to her knee with a heavy huff.

"I'm confused, Miranda. What does that mean exactly?"

"Jack Randall is looking to fill a position for his new nonprofit organization. I know you're familiar with Libraries Without Borders, which is similar. Jack is specifically looking for a traveling librarian to work with libraries and school districts to set up a reading-with-dogs program. With your history with Frank, I felt it would be the perfect match."

"Thank you, Miranda, but I'm confused about why you'd recommend me for a position after you didn't feel I was qualified for one at your library."

"Look, Ms. Gardner, it's the holiday season, and I, for one, believe in miracles. Honestly, the position here wouldn't have been a good fit for you and Frank. You can offer so much more to patrons with Jack's organization. I suppose, if I were being candid, that as soon as we started chatting during the interview, I knew you could find a better job." Miranda whispered something off the phone. "Sorry about that. See, yesterday evening, when you received the call from Tina about us going with another applicant, she was supposed to mention that I'd be calling you today. And when Tina got into work this morning, well, I had to call you right away."

"Thank you, Miranda." April set her mug on the coffee table.

"It's my pleasure. Please expect a call from Jack sometime today. He's looking to set up an interview with you and, of course, Frank. His organization is based out of California, only a four-hour drive from Woolsey. However, since you'll be traveling, there's a possibility that you could work from your home base since Jack's looking to take it completely virtual once it's established."

"Thank you so much, Miranda." She gave the bulldog a snuggle before standing up. "Out of curiosity, how do you know so much about this position?"

"Jack is my stepbrother."

"Thank you again for the support, Miranda."

After ending the call, April went to refill her mug and couldn't help but think that everything happened for a reason. However, she had no idea what to expect with this call from Jack. But either way, she wanted to speak with Alex as soon as she had more information.

Chapter 33

Alex

He'd paced the library floor for at least thirty minutes and swore he spotted loops of the wool coming undone in the carpet. April had called him, asked to speak with him right away, but said nothing else, and then left him in suspense for over two hours now.

Alex checked his watch. There was no reason it would take April more than a few minutes to drive or walk from her parents' house to the city center.

"Alexander, there you are." His father waved at him as though he was in a crowd.

"Dad, what's wrong? Is it about April?" Alex hurried toward his father at the entrance of the library.

"April? No, it's about the Sydney. She keeps stopping by to see if I need anything."

"Dad, don't you mean the judge, Elizabeth?"

"I might be going blind, but I can tell the difference between the two women. And when I can't, I can hear the difference." His hand found his heart. "Sydney sounds like Julia Roberts. Elizabeth sounds like a Southern bell." William's hand reached out to Alex's arm. "But she's still driving me crazy."

"Dad," Alex took his father by the hand and assisted him to sit down in the nearby chair, "I never thought about it until now, but—"

"Alexander!"

He faced the library's door. "Trinity, what brings you by?"

"I heard a rumor that you're finally switching things up around here. And I had to come to see for myself."

"Sadly, there is nothing to see yet." He straightened his posture. "However, you're correct. I'm installing an"—he swallowed the lump forming in his throat—"electronic checkout system."

Trinity paused and put her hand on her hip. "No, I already knew about that, Aurora told me. I'm talking about you getting DVDs in." She removed a piece of paper from her purse. "Here." She wiggled it toward him. "It's a request list. Mostly things Jolie would like. And a few for Camden and myself that we've been dying to watch."

Alex hesitantly reached for the paper and nearly choked when he unfolded the long list. "This seems like a lot."

"We don't expect you to get everything at once. Just a little here and there."

"Thank you, that's comforting." Alex slid the list into his pocket.

"Why, Alexander, when did you start being sarcastic?" Trinity smiled.

219

Alex opened his mouth, but no words escaped. He ran his hand through his hair just as Elizabeth came into the library.

"Alexander, I have a favor." The judge approached the fast-forming group. "I heard—"

His hand went forward as though he was a crossing guard for the elementary school crosswalk. "Let me stop you right there, Elizabeth, if I may. I understand word is traveling around town about the upcoming changes, but, for now, I have one focus: April. Have you seen her?"

Before the judge could answer, Charlie and Lillian walked into the library holding hands.

"Did I miss a town meeting?" Alex crossed his arms over his chest.

"We know it's you," Charlie asserted, a smile forming on his mouth.

"Know who is what?" William asked, standing up.

"The Christmas cactus on top of the hill," Lillian added.

"It can't be Alexander, he just had surgery," the judge stated. "He couldn't have hiked up there."

"We don't know how he managed it," Lillian looked at Charlie and then back at Alex. "But we found a hand-made ornament of a book."

"I bet you it was April. She is the other librarian, even if temporarily," Trinity added.

"The mini book had *1984* written on it." Charlie smirked as every head turned to Alex.

"It was him!" Everyone said.

"But how?" William stepped closer to the circle form-ing around his son.

"He went just before his surgery," a female voice came from the entrance to the library. A voice Alex recog-nized.

"April!"

"I thought I saw him out the night before his surgery. A beam from his flashlight crossing over the distance of his property." April had Frank with her and bent down to unclip his leash. "I knew it wasn't William; it was far too late at night. I hadn't been able to sleep and was sitting out on my parents' patio."

April had a cream scarf tucked into the front of her buttoned-up red pea coat and black flats peeked out the bottom of her jeans. Alex wanted to pull her near and hug her, but with half the town gathered around the middle of the library, it was far from appropriate.

"So, if you knew," Alex asked, "why didn't you say anything the night we were at the cacti lighting?"

When April moved toward Alex, he swore the resi-dents parted like Santa's sleigh gliding through a snowy forest. She reached out both hands to him, and he placed his fingertips in her palms.

"Because it caused you to stand close to me, and I didn't want to let the secret out to everyone else." April allowed one of his hands to fall, hanging at his side. "It's more fun that way."

"See, this is why April is great for the library," Trinity stated, and the sound of heads turning against the fabric of jackets seemed to echo throughout the room. "What?

221

It's true. You're all thinking it." She stomped her boot. "Where is Camden? I need him to back me up since everyone's suddenly gone silent."

"Sure, I showed Alex a new direction for the library. But it truly comes down to him, and he wanted to change." April turned her back to the Christmas tree. "But you know they won't happen overnight. And Trinity, shame on you. I know you already gave Alex your movie list."

"Why do you keep calling my son Alex? It's *Alexander*." William removed his vet's hat.

"I don't mind it being shortened. I told April to call me Alex."

A whispered chorus of "Ohhh" came from the residents.

"We only wish there was a way for both of you to run the library," the judge mentioned.

"That's why I'm here. I was offered a job." April squeezed Alex's hand.

"I thought you said the job in Olympia went to another candidate?"

"It did. But a woman from the hiring panel has a stepbrother . . ." April glanced around. "It's a long story, but just this afternoon, I was offered a position. Actually, Frank and I were offered a dream position."

The residents all turned to Frank, watching him as he laid on the blanket next to the desk, and then back to April.

"That still means you're leaving Woolsey," Alex noted.

April shook her head. "Yes and no. See, I need to be out in California for the first six months, to work directly with the owner, Jack. It's near San Diego, so only about a four-hour drive. Then, once everything is running smoothly, I'll be traveling to other libraries all over the United States, with Frank in tow."

"I don't see how this is good news." Alex let go of April's hand.

"My home base can be anywhere I want. I'll travel one week a month, and the rest will be virtual." April smiled. "The problem is I know my parents will want their space, so I'll need to find someplace to stay in the summer until I can figure out something more permanent."

Alex couldn't offer they move in together or even think about any other future steps. It was far too soon, but he had no idea what to say.

"You could stay at Sydney's house," the judge suggested. "Remember, she goes up north every summer."

"That's a perfect idea. I'll ask her when I go pick up my parents' mail today."

"Hey, Short Stuff Gardner."

Alex watched Lucas enter the library, making a beeline for April.

"Lucas," April said as the room remained silent. "What can we do for you?"

"I'm only looking for you." He pointed and winked at the same time.

April crossed her arms and leaned back in her stance. "Oh, Lucas. I hate to do this to you, but you really can't take a hint."

Lucas glanced around at the residents. "A hint about what? I'm here to see if you've got plans for this evening. We can go on a date."

"Sorry, I have to wash my hair tonight."

The judge muffled a laugh as R. J. bumped her side.

"It doesn't look dirty." Lucas peered at the top of April's head. "I guess another time then." He gave a nod and headed back out of the library.

"I think Alexan—*Alex*—and April need a little time alone," William stated.

"Right, yes, absolutely," Charlie said.

Alex and April waited for the residents to file out the library door, and then she took him by the hand and led him to the two plum chairs nearest the lighted Christmas tree.

"Alex, I thought this would make you happy." April folded her hands into her lap.

"You're leaving. For six months."

"Are you saying you don't think we should try a relationship?"

"Long distance?" Alex couldn't look her in the eyes, knowing it would make everything much harder.

"I can come back on my days off, or you could come out. Once your back is one hundred percent."

"That's true."

"I figured you might like to start our relationship long distance. It would give you more time to get used to everything changing. I know you're not big on change."

"I can handle change." He removed Trinity's movie list from his pocket. "See." He waved it in the air. "Movies."

"What's wrong then? I thought you'd be happier for me. I won't be a threat to your job anymore."

Alex set the list on the end table between the two chairs and stood to pace back and forth in front of the Christmas tree.

"Alex?" April asked, her voice sounding miles away. "Alex?"

He stopped and refocused to see April standing in front of him, the glow of white lights behind her. When he took her hands into his, he raised them to his chest and pressed them against it. "If someone had told me that change meant falling in love with you, then I would've changed my entire world years ago."

"You—" She blinked long and pressed her lashes together tight. "You're falling in love with me?"

He pressed his lips together, and his brow creased in the middle. "Yes, I am. And I'm not sorry. I hope that you understand. I'm only being honest, and if that sca—"

"Alex, I love you. I'm not falling at all. I had the biggest crush on you in high school. This entire holiday season has been more than I could ever dream of."

He didn't know what to say. For the first time, he couldn't think of any words. Everything he tried to say ended up in a jumble of letters.

April let go of his hands and wrapped them around his neck, pulling Alex's lips to hers. And he enveloped his arms around her waist, wanting desperately to pick her up, but that would have to wait until his back was fully healed. When they parted, his knees wobbled, and Frank approached.

"We wondered if you had any plans for Christmas?" April looked down at the bulldog and then back at Alex.

"I do. I'm sorry. I have an entire library to make changes to. You see, this girlfriend of mine is very sought-after and will be leaving soon. I must spend every second I can with her and her dog, soaking up all her creativity and knowledge."

"She sounds amazing." April took his hand. "Lucky you."

Alex brought her hand to his lips and kissed the top of it. "Lucky me."

Epilogue

The following Christmas

"Thank you for your help, Elizabeth." Alex straightened his holly berry tie in the computer monitor's reflection on the library desk.

"She's going to love it." The judge eyed the room. "You've outdone yourself this year with the Christmas decorations. And the tree, I'm surprised it cleared the ceiling." She gazed up at the eight-foot-tall noble fir decorated in classic ornaments and strung with cranberries and twinkling white lights, and then towards the dinosaur.

"Do you think she'll like it?" He motioned with his head at the seven-foot-tall blown up dinosaur with a Santa hat. "See, I'm expanding my horizons."

Elizabeth grinned. "Even Christmas needs a dinosaur."

"Alright," he checked his watch, "she should be here any minute. Is everyone ready?"

"Yes, they're all in position." Elizabeth squeezed his shoulder and hurried into her spot.

"She's here. April's here," Charlie said, running into the library.

Alex swallowed hard and closed his eyes for a second. When he opened them, April came through the entrance to the library with Frank at her side.

"How wonderful to have you back," William said, and handed April a hardcover book.

She took it and glanced down. "What's going on, William? And why is this book covered in a brown paper sack?" She looked down again at the novel in her hand. "Wait." She dropped Frank's leash and ran her hand over the book as though she was mistaken. "I see the word *will*."

April looked up, and Charlie appeared from around a bookshelf. He handed her another book, and she took it with hesitation. "What's happening?"

She looked at the second book, now atop the first. "This book is covered, too, but it says *you*. Alex, why are these books covered, except for one word?" April giggled, and she watched Alex give Frank a welcome pat on the head.

The judge stepped forward and held out a book. April took it. "*Marry*." She tilted her head.

Trinity smiled and handed over another book.

She took it and read, "*Me*."

Alex was standing next to the Christmas tree when she looked up, the final book in hand. And when April approached him, he handed over the novel.

"This one only has a question mark. Why—" Then April gasped, going back through the stack of five books she held. *"Will you marry me?"*

Alex lowered to his left knee and removed the cherry-red velvet box from his back pocket. He eased opened the case and presented April with a horizontal baguette ring. "Will you do me the honor of being my forever librarian? To show me which books are great and which ones to skip? And, most importantly, will you marry me?"

The books in April's hands crashed to the carpet below, and she brought her hands together in a praying motion at her lips. "I've never wanted anything more in my entire life than to be your wife."

Alex rose and removed the ring from the box, sliding it onto her right finger. She then took it and put it on the correct finger as the residents moved toward the tree and the newly engaged couple.

"See, already learning." Alex shook his head and pulled her into a hug.

Everyone clapped, and Frank let out a bark before lying back down on the raised bed that Alex had set out for him in the bulldog's favorite spot of the library, next to the classic desk in the town they all called home.

Thank you for visiting Woolsey, Arizona. I hope you enjoyed your time getting to know the residents and the desert lifestyle. The best thing about a novel is you can come back anytime you wish and don't ever have to worry about change.

Did you LOVE, LIKE, or DISLIKE this novel? Let me know by leaving a review, please and thank you.

Acknowledgments

A big hug to my **PAWS Readers** ~ Sam Alvarez, Robin Batterson, Rachel Blackburn, Carol Harris, JoAnna Mc-Garvie, JoDena Pysher, Elaine Sapp, Carrie Thompson, and Lisa Wetzel.

Thank you to my editor Krista Dapkey for your amazing editing skills.

Thank you to my returning readers who have followed my career and been utterly supportive: Piepie Baltz, Sherri Bailey, Sandy Herzog, Betty Mitchell, Durene Adams, Sandy Ebbinga, Annette G. Anders, Lissa Ruck, Patty Bulick, and Lisa Small. Y'all are always so excited to read my latest novel and I love you for it!

Thank you to my dad, Greg, for reading yet another romance novel that he REALLLLY didn't want to read. Thank you for all the tutoring, Sylvan Learning Center, and Hooked on Phonics. You made sure I had what I needed to overcome my reading and writing struggles.

And thank you, Ransom, for drooling on my laptop.

About the Author

Savannah Hendricks (born in California, raised in Washington, and resides in Arizona) is a full-time social worker and fills as much of her weekends as possible with writing. She loves all things dog-related and has a passion for red wine. Savannah enjoys gardening, baking, and creating yummy recipes. You'll often find her hollering at the TV during restoration shows when they paint over red bricks.

If you'd love a digital personalized autograph or bookplate, you can request one by visiting: savannahhendricks.com
Please discover more about Savannah by interacting with her on:

Instagram: savannahhendricks_author
Facebook: AuthorSavannahHendricks

Also By Savannah

Adding heart & humor to your reading journey

GRAB YOUR BOOKS HERE

<u>Humorously Wholesome Romance</u>
Route to Romance
A Desert Restoration, A Desert Romance, and *A Desert Rivalry* (A Hearts of Woolsey series)
A Christmas Rental
Grounded in January (Award-Winning)
Grounded in July
To Work Out or to Wed

<u>Heartfelt Coming of Age</u>
The Album (Award Finalist)

SAVANNAH HENDRICKS

I Adopted My Mom at the Bus Station (Award-Winning)

<u>Meaningful Picture Books</u>
Winston Versus the Snow (Award-Winning)
Nonnie and I (Available in English, Spanish & Bilingual)